ELVIS

ALL SHOOK UP

ELVIS

ALL SHOOK UP

Stories and Insights from FAMILY MEMBERS,
JOURNALISTS, AND THOSE WHO WERE THERE

With an introduction by ROY BLOUNT, JR.

STERLING
New York

STERLING
New York

An Imprint of Sterling Publishing
387 Park Avenue South
New York, NY 10016

ISBN 978-1-4027-8418-7

Distributed in Canada by Sterling Publishing
$^{c}/_{o}$ Canadian Manda Group, 165 Dufferin Street
Toronto, Ontario, Canada M6K 3H6

For information about custom editions, special sales, and premium
and corporate purchases, please contact Sterling Special Sales at 800-805-5489
or specialsales@sterlingpublishing.com.

Manufactured in the United States of America

2 4 6 8 10 9 7 5 3 1

www.sterlingpublishing.com

For the fans.

CONTENTS

INTRODUCTION

By Roy Blount, Jr.

F AT ELVIS, OKAY. BUT *OLD* ELVIS? SEVENTY-SEVEN, HE WOULD be by now. Other icons born in 1935 are still around and reasonably (if not unreasonably) well-preserved: Jerry Lee Lewis, Johnny Mathis, Loretta Lynn, Julie Andrews, Sandy Koufax, Woody Allen. But who can imagine Elvis *mature*, even? Of all American legends, he was the biggest baby.

Dead Elvis, I witnessed myself. The only time I saw him in person, he was forty-two and in the coffin. In the foyer of Graceland, he lay in state. Many thousands of fans, a good percentage of them on the verge, at least, of tears, and all of them undoubtedly sweating in the August heat, were waiting three or four abreast in a line stretching for blocks and blocks down Elvis Presley Boulevard. A press credential got me in ahead of the masses. Elvis was surrounded by glowering bodyguards who kept everyone moving briskly, determined as they were to keep anyone from sneaking a snapshot. So I went through twice. The *National Enquirer* did publish a photo, but if it wasn't fake, it was touched up prettier than the face I saw.

People have often asked whether it occurred to me that I was looking at a mannequin that Elvis had arranged to be placed there so he could begin life anew. *Of course* that had occurred to me, and we now know that Elvis had indeed made a plan, years earlier, to exchange identities with someone terminally ill, so that "Elvis" could pass away and let the old boy who had become Elvis live—maybe withdraw to "a little shack on a farm and just forget fame and fortune and all the craziness that goes with it," as Linda Thompson says the two of them often thought would be fun.

But that scheme fizzled. One reason, I'll bet, was that Elvis liked his own body too much—he abused it by indulging, not denying it—to let it waste away even by proxy. And one reason I am sure he was dead is that even in his puffy, self-parodying forties, Elvis had too much pride in his appearance to contrive to be represented as downright ugly in his most dramatic hour. He could have afforded a much handsomer simulacrum of himself than the bloated, scowling figure I saw. Elvis in the coffin looked not only dead but all out of sorts about it. He looked like he was sulking.

"Before Elvis there was nothing," said John Lennon. I don't remember it that way exactly. I had a pretty good year when I was twelve. But it's true that before Elvis, the closest thing to a youth culture that I can recall was Eddie Haskell on *Leave It to Beaver*, who thought, at least, that he was putting things over on grown-ups. Elvis was nothing like Eddie. Elvis's politeness to elders was genuine, and he was too impulsive and befuddled to connive. Or to grow up. "May you stay forever young," Bob Dylan sang, and "I was so much older then, I'm younger than that now." Yeah, yeah, but Dylan grew up, in his own dried-up but cannily myth-preserving way. If you don't age, you die.

Elvis lived for his mother; then she died, and he sobbed uncontrollably for days. He never got over the loss of that plump, unconditional lady who baby-talked with him. Girls could be persuaded to lull him to sleep with such talk, but that wasn't the same. We have Richard Beymer instead of Elvis in *West Side Story* because Elvis let himself be dominated and sold short by his father figure, Colonel Parker. His sexuality (see Peggy Lipton's account in this book) seems to have been that of a lucky 1950's fourteen-year-old. He overate yummy but constipating food, followed by laxatives that required him to wear diapers, and he gobbled handfuls of otherwise infantilizing pills until his body gave up hope that he would ever take care of it. When he'd been hospitalized at least five times in order to detox, friends tried to talk him into giving up the drugs. "I'm going to do what I want to do," he said, "and that's the way it is." He got as far as adolescence, stayed there for twenty years, and then regressed.

Along the way, he sang "That's All Right" and "All Shook Up," and so on and so on, and he sang and danced his ass off to "Jailhouse Rock." You have to love Ann-Margret's account of their spontaneous choreography: "We looked at each other move and saw virtual mirror images. When Elvis thrust his pelvis, mine slammed forward too. When his shoulder dropped, I was down there with him. When he whirled, I was already on my heel." Maybe nobody with any capacity for prudence could have had the kinds of highs Elvis had in his twenties. Who knew, at the time, that such highs were up there, at least for a common man?

As of this writing, Keith Richards has lived twenty-seven more years than Elvis did. When Keith was a boy he caught Elvis singing on the radio. He had already heard Little Richard's "Long Tall Sally," but Elvis's "Heartbreak Hotel" was "the one that really turned me on, like an explosion. . . . That was the stunner. I'd never heard . . . anything like it. . . . It was almost as if I'd been waiting for it to happen. When I woke up the next day, I was a different guy." But by the time Elvis joined the army, Keith decided he'd "gone wonky." The Beatles came to pay homage to Elvis and found him defensive and uncool. Who was he going to hang out with, other than his Memphis stooges? There was no one in his category. He had a lot to do with creating a generation, but he wasn't part of it. He was a generation unto himself, not a beatnik, not a hippie. He was sort of the opposite of the Dutch boy who plugged the hole in the dike. Elvis unplugged the dike of the fifties, and other people's satisfaction swept him out to sea. After he died, Jerry Lee Lewis (who was too rowdy to be Elvis's buddy) said, "Elvis had to wait till the world was asleep, to ride his motorcycle."

"For Elvis," writes Bobbie Ann Mason, "the burning question was 'Why am I Elvis? Why was I picked to be Elvis Presley?' He couldn't imagine that his tremendous popularity might have been simply the result of talent and ambition and hard work and random circumstances." Things would have been simpler if he'd gone full-bore gospel—but with those hips? Had to be rock and roll, and behold: Rock and roll came to be. And so he pursued mysticism, died reading *The Scientific Search for the Face of Jesus.* (You can get a used copy online for $120.) "He was innocently authentic," Mason observes, "but he craved the inauthentic, as country people, who are so close—uncomfortably close—to what is starkly real, often do." If you had sat next to him on a bus and got to talking about the meaning of life, and you didn't know who he was, you would have thought he was missing something upstairs. Artists sacrifice—or lack—whatever would prevent others from showing their stuff. Maybe they don't know how to do anything else. If Elvis's dopamine threshold hadn't been where it was, he wouldn't have been the Hillbilly Cat.

He was a different guy from birth, odd man in at the death of his twin. But he was the essence of accessible. We are still able to enjoy his highs along with him as we tut-tut his lows. If you go to Graceland, you will see that the wall outside the property is covered with graffiti gushing total acceptance: "Rhode Island loves Elvis." "Explorer Scouts love Elvis." "Griff and Myrnalynda love Elvis." It's not an emotion that anybody has to give any thought to, which I guess is how love ought ideally to be. So why do we keep trying to think about Elvis? (Even *he* kept trying to think about Elvis.) Can't we just let him be?

I just had a thought—*here we go again*—but no, this is not so much a thought as an impression, or something. I have been struck dumb by unexpectedly bumping into cultural figures I admired but never expected to meet: Jack Benny, Ray Bolger, Alice Munro, Cab Calloway. I must have struck them as rude, because I couldn't even stammer. But with Elvis, somehow or other . . .

Maybe what I was about to say isn't true. But no, I think it is. I was about to say that if I were to encounter Elvis out of the blue, either down here, the seventy-seven-year-old Elvis, or in heaven, Elvis in his prime—oh, sure, I would come to marvel at the wondrousness of it all, but my first reaction, I do believe, would just be to say, "Hey, Elvis."

THE START OF A
REVOLUTION

From *The Fifties*, Chapter 31[*]

By David Halberstam

David Halberstam was a Pulitzer Prize-winning journalist and author who wrote about the Vietnam War, the civil rights movement, American culture, and sports. His bestselling *The Fifties* tracks the trends and notable figures of the decade, including rock and roll, fast food, the birth control pill, Marlon Brando, the Beats, and, of course, Elvis. This chapter excerpt recaps the early days of Elvis and describes the forces and energy behind Elvis's improbable rise to superstardom.

T HE SUPREME COURT RULING ON BROWN V. BOARD OF EDUCATION, which occurred in the middle of the decade, was the first important break between the older, more staid America that existed at the start of the era, and the new, fast-paced, tumultuous

• • •

America that saw the decade's end. The second was Elvis Presley. In cultural terms, his coming was nothing less than the start of a revolution. Once, in the late sixties, Leonard Bernstein, the distinguished American composer and conductor, turned to a friend of his named Dick Clurman, an editor at *Time* magazine. They were by chance discussing political and social trends. "Elvis Presley," said Bernstein, "is the greatest cultural force in the twentieth century." Clurman thought of the sultry-faced young man from the South in tight clothes and an excessive haircut who wiggled his body while he sang about hound dogs. Bernstein's statement seemed a bit much. "What about Picasso?" he began, trying at the same time to think of other major cultural forces of the century. "No," Bernstein insisted, and Clurman could tell that he was deadly serious, "it's Elvis. He introduced the beat to everything and he changed everything— music, language, clothes, it's a whole new social revolution—the Sixties comes from it. Because of him a man like me barely knows his musical grammar anymore." Or, as John Lennon, one of Elvis's admirers, once said, "Before Elvis there was nothing."

If he was a revolutionary, then he was an accidental one, an innately talented young man who arrived at the right place at the right time. He had no political interests at all, and though his music symbolized the coming together of black and white cultures into the mainstream in a way that had never happened before, that seemed to hold little interest for him. Though much of his music had its roots among blacks, he, unlike many young white musicians, seemed to have little interest in the black world and the dramatic changes then taking place there. Indeed, he often seemed to have little interest in music at all. What he really wanted from the start was to go to Hollywood and be a movie star like James Dean or

Marlon Brando, a rebel up on the screen. It was almost as if the music that shook the world was incidental. Brando and Dean were his role models, and when he finally got to Hollywood and met Nicholas Ray, who had directed Dean in *Rebel Without a Cause,* he got down on his knees and started reciting whole pages from the script. He had, Ray realized, seen *Rebel* at least a dozen times and memorized every line that Dean spoke. If he would never rival Brando and Dean as a movie actor, he learned from them one critical lesson: never to smile. That was the key to their success, he was sure. He was sure he could manage the same kind of sultry good looks they had. As a teenager he spent hours in front of a mirror working on that look, and he used it to maximum effect, later, in his own appearances.

Sam Phillips, Memphis recording man, enthusiast of black music, had been looking for years for someone like Elvis—a white boy who could sing like a black boy and catch the beat of black music. Elvis, Phillips later said, "knew I was there a long time before he finally walked into my studio. I saw that Crown Electric Company truck that he was driving pull up a number of times outside the studio. He would sit in it and try to get his courage up. I saw him waiting there long before he got the nerve to come in." Elvis Presley walked into that studio in the summer of 1953. He had been sent there by another talent scout, who had not wanted anything to do with him—and those awful pegged pants, the pink and black clothes. He was an odd mixture of a hood—the haircut, the clothes, the sullen, alienated look; and a sweet little boy—curiously gentle and respectful, indeed willing and anxious to try whatever anyone wanted. Everyone was sir or ma'am. Few young Americans, before or after, have looked so rebellious and been so polite.

Sam Phillips immediately liked Presley's early greaser style. The clothes came from Lansky's, a store more likely to be visited by flashy black men around town then by young white males. "And the sideburns, I liked that too. Everyone in town thought *I* was weird, and here was this kid and he was as weird as I was," Phillips recalled. There is some dispute as to whether Sam Phillips was in the studio the day that Elvis first walked in. Marion Kreisker, Phillips's secretary, believes he was not, and in her account she takes credit for his first recording. Phillips insisted that he *was* there, and that while Ms. Kreisker may have spoken to him first, he actually cut Presley's first disc. "It's a very expensive piece of equipment and I wasn't about to let a secretary use it," he noted. "What do you sing?" Marion Kreisker asked. "I sing all kinds," she remembered him answering. "Well, who do you sound like?" she prodded. "I don't sound like nobody," he replied. He told her he wanted to cut a record for his mother's birthday, which was still several months away.

So he sang into Phillips's little record machine, getting his three dollars' worth. He sang two Ink Spots songs, "My Happiness" and "That's When Your Heartaches Begin." Presley himself was disappointed with the results. "Sounded like someone beating on a bucket lid," he said years later. Sam Phillips later said that he heard Elvis sing and thought to himself, *Oh man, that is distinctive. There is something there, something original and different.*

Sam Phillips listened to Presley a few times and was sure that Elvis had some kind of special talent, but he just wasn't sure what it was. He was not a particularly good guitar picker, but there was a sound almost buried in there that was distinctive. Part of it was Elvis's musical promiscuity: He did not really know who he was. After one frustrating session, Phillips asked him what he could do. "I can do anything," he said. He sang everything: white, black, gospel, country, crooners. If anything, thought Phillips, he seemed to see himself as a country Dean Martin. "Do you have any friends you woodshed with?" Phillips asked him. Woodshedding was a term to mean musicians going off and working together. Elvis replied, no. Phillips said he had two friends, and he called Scotty Moore at his brother's dry-cleaning shop. Moore was an electric-guitar player and Phillips suggested he and Bill Black, a bassist, work out with Elvis. They were to try to bring forth whatever it was that was there. Elvis, Moore thought—that's a science fiction name. After a few weeks of working together, the three of them went to Phillips's studio to record. Phillips by chance entered the date in his log: July 5, 1954. For a time the session did not go particularly well. Elvis's voice was good, but it was too sweet, thought Phillips. Then Elvis started picking on a piece, by a famed black bluesman named Arthur Crudup, called "I'm All Right, Mama." Crudup was a Mississippi blues singer who had made his way to Chicago with an electric guitar. He was well known within the narrow audience for black blues. He had recorded this particular song seven years earlier, and nothing had happened with it. Suddenly, Elvis Presley let go: He was playing and jumping around in the studio like all the gospel singers, black and white, he had watched onstage. Soon his two sidemen joined him. "What the hell are you doing?" Phillips asked. Scotty Moore said he didn't know. "Well find out real quick and don't lose it. Run through it again and let's put it on tape," Phillips said. They turned it into a record. Having covered a black blues singer for one side, it seemed only fitting to use Presley's version of bluegrass singer Bill Monroe's "Blue Moon of Kentucky" on the other.

Country blended with black blues was a strain that some would come to call rock-a-billy, something so powerful that it would go right to the center of American popular culture. Crudup, one of the legendary pure black blues singers of his time, was not thrilled by the number of white singers who seemed to make so much money off the work he had pioneered. "I was makin' everybody rich and I was poor," he once said. "I was born poor, I live poor, and I'm going to die poor." Bo Diddley, the great black rocker, was more philosophical. Someone later asked Diddley if he thought Presley had copied his style. "If he copied me, I don't care—more power to him," Diddley said. "I'm not starving."

Phillips was sure the record was a winner and he sent it to a local disc jockey named Dewey Phillips (no relation), who had a show called *Red, Hot and Blue*, on WHBQ. He was very big with the young white kids—Elvis himself had listened faithfully almost every night since he was fourteen years old. Dewey Phillips played traditional white artists all the time, but just as regularly, he played the great black singers, blues and gospel. "Dewey was not white," the black blues singer Rufus Thomas once said in the ultimate accolade. "Dewey *had* no color." Dewey and Sam, spiritually at least, were kin. If Sam was a man who subscribed to very few local conventions, then Dewey openly liked to flaunt them. He had ended up at WHBQ, as much as anything else, by being very unsuccessful at anything else he tried. He came from Adamsville, in west Tennessee. As a boy he had loved listening to black music, although he had been assured by his elders that it was the work of the devil. He had visited Memphis as a boy once when he was ten to sing in a Baptist church choir. The lady in charge had taken them to their hotel, the Gayoso, and explained to them that there were two rules: first, they were not to order from room service, since they would eat at churches; second, they were not to wander over to Beale Street. Dewey immediately took a younger boy and went to Beale Street. It had not disappointed him, with its rich black life and music. Eventually, after serving in the army, he came back home and migrated to Memphis. There he had started out working in a bakery. He was fired when he convinced the other bakers that instead of making the regular bread, they should all make loaves shaped like little gingerbread men. Baking, obviously, was not his calling. He next went to work as a stockboy for the W. T. Grant store downtown. There he managed to get himself in the store's music department and soon was beaming his department's records over loudspeakers into the street at top volume. That, of course, stopped downtown traffic. He also accompanied them with his own patter by plugging a microphone into the store's record player. He had invented himself as a disc jockey. All he needed was a radio station.

At the time Memphis had a radio show called *Red, Hot and Blue*, which consisted of fifteen minutes of popular music on WHBQ. Dewey Phillips often told friends that he would do the show for nothing if they would let him try. He went down to WHBQ, asked for a job, and miraculously got it. He was so different, so original, that the management did not know at first whether to fire him or expand the show; within a year he had three hours to himself. He was, in the words of his friend Stanley Booth, both brilliant and terrible as a disc jockey. He could not read a line of copy, and he could not put a record on without scratching it. But he had perfect taste in the music that young people wanted to hear. Soon he was the conduit that hip young white Memphis kids used to hear black music with its powerful beat. Political boss Ed Crump might keep the streets and schools and public buildings segregated, but at night Dewey Phillips integrated the airwaves. Daddy-O-Dewey, he was soon called. Phrases he tossed away casually at night on his show became part of the teenage slang of Memphis the next day. Stumble he might while doing the commercials (and he might even do commercials for people who had not bothered to buy time—he was always suggesting that his listeners go out and buy a fur-lined Lincoln, even if Lincoln was not an advertiser), but he was wildly inventive.

There were always surprises on his show. He loved having contests as well, and all three of his sons were named during radio contests. He was a man driven by a kind of wonderful madness and an almost sweet desire to provoke the existing establishment, and to turn the world gently upside down. Memphis in those days still had a powerful movie censor, Lloyd Binford, and when Binford had banned an early teen movie, Phillips had played its theme song, Bill Haley's "Rock Around the Clock," and dedicated it to Binford: "And this goes out to Lloyd Binford. . . . How you *doin'*, Lloyd? . . . Anyway . . ." There he was in clean, well-ordered Memphis, tapping beneath the polite, white surface into the wildness of the city.

On one occasion he decided he wanted to find out how large his listenership was. Nothing as clumsy as demographic polls for Dewey Phillips, particularly since Memphis had just won an award for being the nation's quietest city—instead, he just told everyone listening to him to blow their horns at 9 P.M. If they were in their cars they could blow their horns, and if they were in their homes they should go out to their cars and blow the horns. At 9:05 the police chief called the station and told him, "Dewey, you just can't do this to us—the whole city's gone crazy, everybody out there is blowing horns." So Dewey Phillips went back on the air and told his listeners what the chief had just told him. "So I can't tell you to blow your horns at 11:30." The faithful went back out and blew their horns at 11:30.

Dewey Phillips had, in his friend Sam Phillips's words, "a

platinum ear" and was connected to young listeners like no other adult. Therefore, he was the first person Sam Phillips thought of when he had Elvis's first disc. Dewey agreed to play it. The night he did, Elvis was so nervous that he went to a movie by himself. The two songs were such a success that all Dewey Phillips did that night was flip the record back and forth. The switchboard started lighting up immediately. Finally the disc jockey decided he wanted to interview Elvis on the air, and he called Sam Phillips and told him to bring the boy in. The Presleys did not have a phone, but Sam called over to their neighbors and they got Elvis's mother. Gladys and Vernon Presley had to go looking for their elusive son in the movie theater. "Mama, what's happening?" he asked. "Plenty, son," she answered, "but it's all good." Off they went to the station. There he was introduced to Dewey Phillips, who was going to interview him. "Mr. Phillips," he said. "I don't know nothin' about being interviewed." "Just don't say nothing' dirty," Phillips said. So they talked. Among other things, Phillips deftly asked Elvis where he had gone to high school, and Elvis answered Humes, which proved to the entire audience that yes, he was white. At the end Phillips thanked him. "Aren't you going to interview me?" Presley asked. "I already have," Phillips said.

ELVIS ARON PRESLEY WAS BORN IN THE HILL COUNTRY OF NORTHEAST Mississippi in January 1935. It was a particularly poor part of a poor region in a nation still suffering through the Depression; in contrast to other parts of Mississippi, it was poor cotton land, far from the lush Delta 150 miles further west. Yet the local farmers still resolutely tried to bring cotton from it (only when, some thirty years later, they started planting soybeans did the land become valuable), and it was largely outside of the reach of the industrial revolution. Presley's parents were typical country people fighting a daily struggle for survival. Gladys Smith until her marriage and her pregnancy operated a sewing machine and did piecework for a garment company, a rare factory job in the area. Vernon Presley—a man so poorly educated that he often misspelled his own name, signing it Virnon—was the child of a family of drifters and was employed irregularly, taking whatever work he was offered: perhaps a little farming, perhaps a little truck driving. He lived on the very fringes of the American economy; he was the kind of American who in the thirties did not show up on government employment statistics. At the time of their marriage Gladys was twenty-one, four years older than Vernon. Because they were slightly embarrassed by the fact that she was older, they switched ages on their marriage certificate. Elvis was one of twins, but his brother, Jessie Garon Presley, was stillborn, a death that weighed heavily on both mother and son.

When Gladys became pregnant, Vernon Presley borrowed $180 from Orville Bean, a dairy farmer he worked for, and bought the lumber to build his family a two-room cabin. The cabin was known as a shotgun shack—because a man could stand at the front door and fire a shotgun and the pellets would go straight out the back door. When Elvis was two years old, Vernon Presley was picked up for doctoring a check from Bean. It had been an ill-conceived, pathetic attempt to get a few more dollars, at most. Friends of Vernon's pleaded with Bean not to press charges. They would make up the difference. But Bean was nothing if not rigid, and he held firm against their pleas. Vernon Presley could not make bail, and he waited seven months in the local jail before the trial even took place. He was convicted and sent to Parchman prison in the middle of the Depression for two and a half years. It was a considerable sentence for a small crime, but those were hard times. When he came out times were still hard; he worked in a lumberyard and then for one of the New Deal aid programs for the unemployed, the WPA.

During World War Two he got a job doing defense work in Memphis, eighty miles away. That at least was steady work, even if he was away from home much of the time. After the war, returning veterans had priority for any jobs. Vernon had no skills and was soon out of work again. In the late forties the new affluence rolling quickly across much of the country barely touched people like Vernon and Gladys Presley. They were poor whites. Their possibilities had always been limited. They were people who lived on the margin. Religion was important to them, and when Elvis was nine he was baptized in the Pentecostal church. As a symbol of Christian charity, he was supposed to give away some of his prized possessions, so he gave his comic books to other children.

Because a city like Memphis held out more hope of employment, Vernon Presley moved his family to Memphis in the late forties. There he took a job in a paint factory for $38.50 a week. They had made the move, Elvis said later, because "we were broke, man, broke." The family was still so poor that it had to live in federal housing—the projects as they were known. The Presleys paid thirty-five dollars a month for rent, the equivalent of a week's salary. To some whites, living in the projects was an unspeakable idea, for it was housing that placed them at the same level as blacks; for the Presleys, the projects were the best housing they had ever had.

Even in a high school of his peers, Elvis Presley was something of a misfit. He went to Humes, an all-white high school where he majored in shop. There was no thought of college for him. Not surprisingly, he was shy and unsure of himself. He was bothered by the

11

way his teeth looked. He worried that he was too short. As an adult he always wore lifts in his shoes. He did, however, have a sense that his hair worked for him. Soon he started using pomade; his style, black clothes, shirt collar up in back, hair pomaded into a major wave, was an early form of American punk. His heroes—Brando and Dean—were narcissistic, so too by nature was he. His social life was so limited that he did not know how to slow-dance with a girl; rather, in the new more modern style, he knew how to dance only by himself. His peers deemed him effeminate and different. Everyone, it seemed, wanted a shot at him, particularly the football players. Years later he would tell a Las Vegas audience, "They would see me coming down the street and they'd say, 'Hot dog! Let's get him! He's a squirrel! He just come down outta the trees!'" His one friend was Red West, a more popular Humes student and a football player. West stopped about five other boys from cutting off Elvis's hair in the boys' room one day. "He looked like a frightened little animal," West said.

The one thing he had was his music. He could play a guitar and play it well. He could not read a note of music, but he had an ear that, in the words of Chet Atkins, the guitarist who supervised many of his early RCA recordings, was not only pure but had almost perfect pitch. He could imitate any other voice he chose. That was his great gift. Some of the other kids suggested he play guitar at a school picnic, and he did, with surprising success. His homeroom teacher asked him to play it at the school variety show. He did, playing the Red Foley country favorite "Old Shep," about a boy and his dog. When the dog dies and goes to heaven, the boy does not feel too badly, for "old Shep has a wonderful friend." For the first time he gained some popularity.

On the surface, the Mississippi he grew up in was a completely segregated world. That was seemingly true even in music. Among the many musical subcultures that flowed across the Mississippi Delta were black rhythm and blues music (called race music in the trade), black gospel, white gospel, which in no small part was imitative of black gospel, and country, or hillbilly, music. Because whites were more influential and affluent than blacks, the last was the dominant strain in the region.

For Elvis Presley, living in a completely segregated world, the one thing that was not segregated was the radio dial. There was WDIA ("the Mother Station of the Negroes," run, of course, by white executives), which was the black station, on which a young white boy could listen to, among other people, the Rev. Herbert Brewster, a powerful figure in the world of Memphis black churches. A songwriter of note, he composed "Move On Up a Little Higher," the first black gospel song to sell over a million copies. What was clear about the black gospel music was that it had a power of its own, missing from the tamer white church music, and that power seemed to come as much as anything else from the beat. In addition there was the immensely popular Dewey Phillips. When Elvis listened to the black radio station at home, his family was not pleased. "Sinful music," it was called, he once noted. But even as Elvis Presley was coming on the scene, the musical world was changing. Certainly, whites had traditionally exploited the work of black musicians, taking their music, softening and sweetening it and making it theirs. The trade phrase for that was "covering" a black record. It was thievery in broad daylight, but black musicians had no power to protect themselves or their music.

As the decade began, there were signs that young white kids were buying black rhythm and blues records; this was happening in pockets throughout the country, but no one sensed it as a trend until early 1951. In that year a man named Lee Mintz, who owned a record store in Cleveland, told a local disc jockey named Alan Freed about this dramatic new trend. Young white kids with more money than one might expect were coming into his store and buying what had been considered exclusively Negro music just a year or two before. Freed, something of a disc jockey and vagabond, had a late-night classical music show, and Mintz was pushing him to switch over to a new show catering exclusively to these wayward kids. Mintz told Freed he knew the reason why the taste was changing: It was all about the beat. The beat was so strong in black music, he said, that anyone could dance to it without a lesson. Mintz promised he would advertise himself on Freed's new program and that he would help find other advertisers if Freed would switch.

Alan Freed was hardly locked into classical music. He was a smart, free-spirited man, who like many of the nation's best disc jockeys, seemed to be two people: one a rather insecure, ordinary person who went angrily through everyday life and the other, a man in front of an open mike who exploded into a secret confident and audacious self before listeners he could not see. His career, at that moment, had not been exactly brilliant. Even within a profession given over to a significant excess of ego, Freed was considered difficult and abrasive by various employers. At one point he had worked at a station in Akron, had asked for a raise, and had been turned down, so he went to a competing station and offered his services. Unfortunately, his contract with the first station had not yet expired; the first station took him to court and a judge ordered him not to broadcast within seventy-five miles of Akron for a year. Such was the life of a disc jockey who has not yet found his special niche. When his period of disbarment expired he eventually showed up in Cleveland.

So when Mintz suggested the new show, he was amenable.

In the summer of 1951, Freed inaugurated *The Moondog Show* on a 50,000-watt clear channel station in Cleveland, a station so powerful it reached a vast area of the Midwest. His success was immediate. It was as if an entire generation of young white kids in that area had been waiting for someone to catch up with them. For Freed it was what he had been waiting for; he seemed to come alive as a new hip personality. He was the Moondog. He kept the beat himself in his live chamber, adding to it by hitting on a Cleveland phone book. He became one of them, the kids, on their side as opposed to that of their parents, the first grown-up who understood them and what they wanted. By his choice of music alone, the Moondog had instantly earned their trust. Soon he was doing live rock shows. The response was remarkable. No one in the local music business had ever seen anything like it before: Two or three thousand kids would buy tickets, and sometimes, depending on the level of talent, thousands of others would be turned away—all for performers that adults had never even heard of.

At virtually the same time, Elvis Presley began to hang out at all-night white gospel shows. White gospel singing reflected the region's schizophrenia: It allowed white fundamentalist groups, whose members were often hard-core segregationists and who wanted nothing to do with black culture—to co-opt the black beat into their white music. Presley gradually got to know some of the gospel singers, and by the time he graduated from high school in 1953, he had decided to become one himself. He was eighteen, with extremely limited options. For a country boy with his background, the possibilities were few: He could drive a truck or hope for a job in a nearby plant—and he could dream of being a singer. Soon he was singing with a local group from his church called the Songfellows. But a few random singing dates were hardly a career, so he was also working at a small plant in Memphis where artillery shell casings were made. By the standards of the time and the region, the pay was not bad—$1.65 an hour—and he made about sixty dollars a week with overtime. Soon he left that job for another that excited him more—driving a truck for Crown Electric. Driving a truck seemed infinitely freer than working in a defense factory. It seemed at that moment he would be driving a truck for the rest of his life. In September 1956, a year after he exploded into the consciousness of his fellow Americans, he tried to explain the secret of his success to a writer for the *Saturday Evening Post*. "I don't know what it is . . . I just fell into it, really. My daddy and I were laughing about it the other day. He looked at me and said, 'What happened, E? The last thing I can remember is I was working in a can factory and you were drivin' a truck,' . . . It just caught us up."

People

PROM DATE OF THE CENTURY

From "Elvis's Prom Date Remembers a Shy Guy in
Blue Suede Shoes," *People Weekly,* July 17, 1989[*]
By Steve Dougherty and Linda Marx

Regis Wilson Vaughn dated Elvis for six months
in the early 1950s. Here, she tells *People Weekly*
(now *People*) what going to the senior prom
with Elvis Presley was like. And yes, she still has
her prom dress.

MILLIONS OF RECENT HIGH SCHOOL GRADUATES MISTILY
remember their senior prom as though it were yesterday
because, for them, it practically *was* yesterday. Regis Wilson
Vaughn, a 50-year-old Fort Lauderdale housewife, can remember
almost everything about her most special prom even though it took
place 36 years ago. She remembers—and still owns—her strapless pink
taffeta dress. She remembers her pink carnation and getting her hair
done for free by a beauty school student. Most of all she remembers

• • •

being picked by a young man who, along with all the other titles he earned during his lifetime, must go down in history as the Prom Date of the Century: Elvis Presley. Then an 18-year-old senior at Memphis's L. C. Humes High School, Elvis wore a dark suit and, his date swears, blue suede shoes. She never got the chance to step on them because Elvis, at that point, didn't dance. "When we entered the Peabody Hotel through a gigantic heart-shaped door and the band was playing, I expected we'd join the other couples dancing," says Vaughn, who by that time had been seeing the incipient hunka hunka burning love for four months. "But Elvis told me he didn't know how to dance. So we sat and talked and drank Cokes all night."

Afterward the boy who would be King took Regis to a local drive-in for burgers, then back to her place. "I kissed Elvis every night from the second date on," says Vaughn. "He was a good kisser. But the nuns at my school told us we shouldn't allow boys to kiss us with their mouths open. So I'll just say Elvis gave me long kisses prom night. You could say we made out. But he never tried to go farther. He wasn't like that." He didn't even come close to suggesting a prom-night visit to the nearest Heartbreak Hotel. "Elvis was the only child of two strict parents," Vaughn says. "Things like that just didn't happen in those days."

Elvis was playing football when he first caught little Regis's eye at the low-income Lauderdale Courts housing project, where both lived. "I thought he was cute," says Vaughn, who was then 14. "I met him later at a birthday party. Elvis asked to take me home. I had never dated then, but I agreed to the ride home in his family car, a 1942 gray Lincoln. He said he wanted to see me again, and I knew I wanted to see him."

Throughout the spring of 1953, the couple dated, going out for malteds and Cokes, attending all-night gospel shows or just spooning on her porch swing. Elvis did sing to her, and it was always the same sad, sweet song—"My Happiness." Later that year Elvis sang it again when he made his first recording, a $4 do-it-yourself acetate that he gave to his mother, Gladys.

"He was so modest," says Vaughn. "He won a variety-show contest at his school and he didn't even tell me about it. I never thought he would become a singer. He talked about finding a job so that he could afford to buy a house for his mama."

One of six children raised by a twice-divorced single mother, Vaughn stopped seeing Elvis a few weeks after the prom, when financial problems forced her family to move from the area. "I didn't want Elvis to know how poor we were," says Vaughn, who didn't even tell him she was leaving. "We moved so many times, I was embarrassed. I didn't tell Elvis because you just didn't call boys in those days. I figured he'd find out I had left by driving by the house and seeing I was gone."

Her family resettled in Fort Lauderdale, and Regis never met Elvis again. In 1956, at 17, she married Herb Vaughn, now 54 and a furniture sales representative. In 1958, they tried to visit Presley, by then a national phenom, after a Miami performance, but security guards kept them out. "I was disappointed," Regis says. "I wanted to say hello and goodbye."

Now a mother of three grown daughters, Vaughn is in school again, studying to be a paralegal at a local community college. She seldom talks about her King-and-I romance. "Who would believe me?" she says. Nonetheless, Herb still gets a little jealous during prime prom season. Why? Because, Regis says with a wink, "He's not as sexy as Elvis."

• • •

AN INTUITIVE MASTER
OF PROVOCATION

From "A Hillbilly Who Wove a Rock-and-Roll
Spell," *New York Times*, July 19, 1987[*]

By Stephen Holden

The famed writer, poet, and *New York Times*
columnist remembers his first impressions of Elvis
in light of a new collection of his earlier music.

O N A COLD SATURDAY NIGHT IN LATE JANUARY 1956, a
seismic shock flickered across American television screens
as Elvis Presley gyrated into national consciousness for
the first time. To a sheltered 14-year-old boy growing up in a New
Jersey town not unlike Springfield, the sanitized suburban paradise
of "Father Knows Best," this loose-limbed hillbilly greaser, with his
pudgy-lipped sneer, shiny hair, flapping legs and hiccupy grunt, had
the impact of an extraterrestrial visitation.

Although word of Elvis Presley had preceded his appearance
that night on "The Dorsey Brothers Stage Show," none of us suburban

• • •

adolescents had yet seen him in action. And when he turned out to be better—and stranger—than we had even imagined, his place in pop history was clinched. Along with his galvanizing physicality, what I remember most clearly was the incredible, brazen self-consciousness of his performance. Far from being carried away by his music, Presley, at 21, was already an intuitive master of provocation who conveyed an amused knowingness. Overnight, thousands of adolescents began imagining themselves as Presley.

By the time RCA Records released his first national hit, "Heartbreak Hotel," a month later, I was a devoted Elvis impersonator who practiced imitating his funny-sexy caricature of sensual abandon in the mirror and for anyone who cared to watch, dreaming that someday the Presley mystique might transform me into someone far more glamorous than a naive ninth-grader from suburbia. When the record came out, I learned every nuance of the slurred, sullen, Southern Presley enunciation that was quickly imitated by rock-and-roll singers across the country. To this day, I don't think anyone has packed more explosive insinuation into the word "baby" than he did in "Heartbreak Hotel."

These early memories of Presley are triggered by RCA Records' release of four albums commemorating the 10th anniversary of the singer's death on Aug. 16, 1977. "The Complete Sun Sessions" (RCA 6414-1-R; LP, cassette, compact disk) collects all the music, including the outtakes, that he cut for Sun Records in Memphis in 1954–55, before being signed by RCA. "The Number One Hits" (6382-1-R; LP, cassette, compact disk), a single disk, collects his 18 No. 1 hits, from "Heartbreak Hotel" (1956) through "Suspicious Minds" (1969). "The Top Ten Hits" (RCA 6383-1-R), a two-disk set, brings together his 38 Top 10 hits, from "Heartbreak Hotel," through "Burning Love" (1972).

"The Memphis Record" (6221-2-R; LP, cassette, compact disk) includes 23 songs recorded in 1969 at the American Studios in Memphis with the producer Chips Moman and a large studio band. These Memphis sessions represented a remarkable, though short-lived, resurgence of energy and commitment by a singer whose career had stagnated throughout most of the 1960's and resumed its downhill slide in the 70's.

Like everything to do with Presley's life and times, the four albums leave deeply contradictory impressions. Presley pioneered the most basic rock-and-roll iconography. He was the original guitar-sporting stud-rebel hero who brought overt male sexual aggression to the American pop mainstream. In "The Sun Sessions," which produced such masterpieces as "Mystery Train," "That's All Right," "Good Rockin' Tonight" and an eerie falsetto version of "Blue Moon," he virtually invented rockabilly with the resourceful help of the producer Sam Phillips, the bassist Bill Black and the lead guitarist Scotty Moore.

These performances are suffused with an aura of mystical exhilaration—the music is almost unearthly. Years later, the singer, whose original idol was the oleaginous crooner, Dean Martin, brought rock-and-roll to Las Vegas and vice versa, fusing the progressive and conservative worlds of musical entertainment. On the one hand, without Elvis, there would probably have been no John Lennon or Bruce Springsteen. On the other, there would also probably be no Tom Jones, Wayne Newton or Julio Iglesias.

For Presley wove the whole unwieldy spectrum of pop singing—country-blues, Italianate crooning, Gospel, soul shouting and honky-tonk yodeling—into an integral personal style. His crowning touch was to accentuate the spontaneously exuberant humor that had always been an ingredient of country and blues singing in a way that seemed to poke fun at his own accomplishment.

Riding a streamlined rock-and-roll beat, the singer's vocal swoops, slurs, hiccups, moans and growls added up to a new pop singing vocabulary that was instantly memorized by scores of imitators. The antithesis of Perry Como's relaxed conversational crooning, Presley's style was fraught with tension and animated by an attitude of self-conscious melodrama. Its essence was a rapid, spontaneous juxtaposition of a whole range of blatantly exaggerated affectations. "Heartbreak Hotel" is the most extreme example of the way Presley substituted an intense gasping punctuation for the smooth bel canto phrasing that Frank Sinatra had refined.

If these commemorative albums bring home once again the revolutionary impact of Presley's singing, they also remind me of why I very quickly stopped wanting to be Presley. While the singer brought plenty of gusto, humor and charisma to his hits after "Heartbreak Hotel," his material was mostly dime-store kitsch that turned his melodramatic mannerisms back on themselves.

Even in the most legendary Presley rockers—"Hound Dog," "Don't Be Cruel" and "Jailhouse Rock," the slick studio rock arrangements and deadening background vocals made him sound like a tamed lion jumping through hoops. In "The Memphis Record," Presley groped toward artistic maturity by emoting with a burly, stern aggression that largely precluded the old joking self-caricature. One hears years of encrusted mannerisms begin to be peeled away as the singer tried to become one with his material. But it was only a beginning. The record is exciting because of the singer's obvious struggle to express authentic emotions that remained stubbornly out of reach.

At their peaks, the greatest popular singers—people like Ray Charles, Frank Sinatra, Billie Holiday, Judy Garland, Hank Williams, Aretha Franklin, Bob Dylan and Stevie Wonder—uncover the bare truths of life. The main truth that Elvis Presley communicated was the tragicomic irony of being Elvis Presley, an icon at 21, idolized and thereafter artistically stunted.

A DEFINITE DANGER
TO THE SECURITY OF
THE UNITED STATES

From Declassified FBI memos
dated 5-16-1956 and 11-7-1956

These are just a few of the 683 pages J. Edgar
Hoover's FBI collected on Elvis Presley and
made available through the Freedom of
Information Act . . . just a few of the many,
many primary documents that show not only
what Elvis did to and for his fans, but also to
and for his detractors. The first document is a
letter written on May 16, 1956, by the editor of
the *La Crosse Register*, a Catholic newspaper
in Louisiana and sent to Hoover. The second
memo is dated November 7, 1956, and relates
the concerns local authorities in Louisville,
Kentucky, had about an upcoming "quote rock
and roll unquote" show.

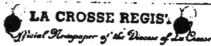

LA CROSSE REGIS
Official Newspaper of the Diocese of La Crosse

THE MOST REV. JOHN P. TREACY, D.D.
BISHOP OF LA CROSSE, PRESIDENT

REV. ANTHONY P. GARNER, EDITOR

PATRICK J. PHELAN, ASSISTANT EDITOR

LEROY JUSTINGER, ADVERTISING MGR.

GENT OFFICE ADDRESS: No. 1
427 HOESCHLER BUILDING
DIAL 2-3923
MAILING ADDRESS
P.O. BOX 822
LA CROSSE, WISCONSIN

May 16, 1956

Mr. Tolson
Mr. Nichols
Mr. Board
Mr. Belmont
Mr. Parsons
Mr. Rosen
Mr. Tamm
Mr. Sizoo
Mr. Winterowd
Mr. Holloman
Miss Gandy

Mr. J. Edgar Hoover
Director
Federal Bureau of Investigation
Washington 25, D.C.

Dear Mr. Hoover,

9-1

Elvis Presley, press-agented as a singer and entertainer, played to two groups of teenagers numbering several thousand at the city auditorium here, Monday, May 14.

As newspaper man, parent, and former member of Army Intelligence Service, I feel an obligation to pass on to you my conviction that Presley is a definite danger to the security of the United States.

Although I could not attend myself, I sent two reporters to cover his second show at 9:30 p.m. Besides, I secured the opinions of others of good judgment, who had seen the show or had heard direct reports of it. Among them are a radio station manager, a former motion picture exhibitor, an orchestra player, and a young woman employee of a radio station who witnessed the show to determine its value. All agree that it was the filthiest and most harmful production that ever came to La Crosse for exhibition to teenagers.

When Presley came on the stage, the youngsters almost mobbed him, as you can judge from the article and pictures enclosed from May 15 edition of the La Crosse TRIBUNE. The audience could not hear his "singing" for the screaming and carrying on of the teenagers.

ENCLOSURE

But eye-witnesses have told me that Presley's actions and motions were such as to rouse the sexual passions of teenaged youth. One eye-witness described his actions as "sexual self-gratification on the stage," – another as "a strip-tease with clothes on." Although police and auxiliaries were there, the show went on. Perhaps the hardened police did not get the import of his motions and gestures, like those of masturbation or riding a microphone. (The assistant district attorney and Captain William Boma also stopped in for a few minutes in response to complaints about the first show, but they found no reason to halt the show.)

SE 15.

After the show, more than 1,000 teenagers tried to gang into Presley's room at the auditorium, then at the Stoddard Hotel. All

28

possible police on duty were necessary at the Hotel to keep
watch on the teenagers milling about the hotel till after 3 a.m.
the hotel manager informed me. Some kept milling about the city
till about 5 a.m.

Indications of the harm Presley did just in La Crosse were
the two high school girls (of whom I have direct personal
knowledge) whose abdomen and thigh had Presley's autograph. They
admitted that they went to his room where this happened. It is
known by psychologists, psychiatrists and priests that teenaged
girls from the age of eleven, and boys in their adolescence are
easily aroused to sexual indulgence and perversion by certain
types of motions and hysteria, -- the type that was exhibited at
the Presley show.

There is also gossip of the Presley Fan Clubs that degenera
into sex orgies. The local radio station WKBH sponsors a club
on the "Lindy Shannon Show."

From eye-witness reports about Presley, I would judge that
he may possibly be both a drug addict and a sexual pervert. In
any case I am sure he bears close watch, -- especially in the
face of growing juvenile crime nearly everywhere in the United
States. He is surrounded by a group of high-pressure agents who
seem to control him, the hotel manager reported.

I do not report idly to the FBI. My last official report
to an FBI agent in New York before I entered the U.S. Army
resulted in arrest of a saboteur (who committed suicide before
his trial). I believe the Presley matter is as serious to U.S.
security. I am convinced that juvenile crimes of lust and
perversion will follow his show here in La Crosse.

I enclose article and pictures from May 15 edition of the
La Crosse TRIBUNE. The article is an excellent example of the
type of reporting that describes a burlesque show by writing
about the drapes on the stage. But the pictures, to say the lea
are revealing. Note, too, that under the Presley article, the
editor sanctimoniously published a very brief "filler" on the
FBI's concern for teenage crime. Only a moron could not see the
connection between the Presley exhibit and the incidence of
teenage disorders in La Crosse.

With many thanks, and with a prayer for God's special
Blessing on your excellent and difficult work for justice and
decency,

Sincerely yours,

DECODED COPY

XXX **Radio** ☐ **Teletype**

FROM LOUISVILLE   11-7-56   NR 071428

TO DIRECTOR   URGENT

ELVIS PRESLEY; BILL HALEY AND HIS COMETS, INFORMATION CONCERNING,
POLICE COOPERATION MATTER. COLONEL CARL E. HEUSTIS, CHIEF OF
POLICE, LOUISVILLE, KENTUCKY, THIS DAY ADVISED THAT ELVIS PRESLEY
AND BILL HALEY AND HIS COMETS, RIVALS FOR THE ATTENTION OF QUOTE
ROCK AND ROLL UNQUOTE FANS, ARE SIMULTANEOUSLY BOOKED FOR APPEAR-
ANCES AT THE JEFFERSON COUNTY ARMORY AND THE KENTUCKY STATE
FAIRGROUND EXPOSITION CENTER NOVEMBER 25 NEXT. COLONEL HEUSTIS
ADVISED HE HAS RECEIVED INFORMATION THAT THERE HAVE BEEN RIOTS
AT JERSEY CITY, NEW JERSEY, ASBURY PARK, NEW JERSEY, SANTA CRUZ,
SANTA JOSE, CALIFORNIA, HARTFORD, CONNECTICUT, AND JACKSONVILLE,
FLORIDA AS RESULT OF SUCH SIMULTANEOUS APPEARANCES. RIOTS
REPORTEDLY RESULTED IN MANY THOUSANDS OF DOLLARS PROPERTY DAMAGE.
COLONEL HEUSTIS REQUESTED INFORMATION FROM THIS BUREAU REGARDING
ANY SUCH RIOTS IN AN EFFORT TO PREVENT SUCH RECURRENCES HERE.
IN VIEW OF THE EXCELLENT COOPERATION BETWEEN LOUISVILLE PD AND
THIS OFFICE IT IS REQUESTED THAT THE BUREAU FURNISH AN AIRTEL
SUMMARY OF ANY INFORMATION APPEARING IN FILES SUITABLE FOR
DISSEMINATION TO COLONEL HEUSTIS.

RECEIVED: 11:05 AM RADIO

     11:22 AM CODING UNIT   MJM

Mr. Rosen

If the intelligence contained in the above message is to be disseminated outside the Bureau, it is suggested that it be suitably paraphrased in order to protect the Bureau's cryptographic systems.

ELVIS, WE MUST LET HER GO

From *The Forgotten Family of Elvis Presley:*
Elvis' Aunt Lois Smith Speaks Out, Chapters 5 and 6[*]

By R. A. Hines Sr.

Lois Smith was married to Gladys Presley's brother, Johnnie Smith, and lived in Memphis with their five children. (Lois also mentions living with Travis, Lorraine, Billy, and Bobby Smith. Travis was Johnnie and Gladys's younger brother. He was married to Lorraine, and Billy and Bobby were two of their children.)

ELVIS BUYS GRACELAND

IN 1957, ELVIS WAS NOW A SUPERSTAR, AND HE PURCHASED THE mansion known all over the world as Graceland. His mother would now have everything she wanted and needed.

• • •

Vernon and Gladys moved into the mansion with Elvis. My mother lived in a small house across the street from Graceland.

Johnnie dropped the kids off at Mother's. He was drinking and didn't want them around. Mother told the kids, "You all go up to Graceland and see Aunt Gladys; she might give you some candy or something." The kids cleaned up and walked up the drive to the mansion. Gladys opened the door and she started in on the kids about the way they were dressed. She said, "Don't come up here looking like that. You go home and put on some good clothes."

The kids told her, "But Aunt Gladys, this is our best." We didn't have the money they now had and it really hurt the kids. They told Johnnie what she had said, and he blew up. Johnnie went to Gladys and told her off. Well, the kids later said they didn't want trouble started over that; it just made them feel bad that she said that.

Elvis started hiring family and friends as bodyguards, security, and all sorts of other positions. Johnnie was hired to work security at the back of Graceland. Travis, Lorraine, Billy and Bobby Smith lived in a white house on the grounds of Graceland, just behind the mansion. Travis was the first gate guard. I would visit Gladys a lot at the mansion. When Johnnie was working and I was off, I would go and stay about all day with Gladys.

I remember once, we were sitting in the back yard, talking. Johnnie was walking the fence.

Gladys said, "I have everything, but what I really want is some grandkids running in this back yard." We talked a lot about Elvis and the past.

I was sitting with Gladys outside one day, and the mailman walked up. He handed Gladys an envelope. Gladys said, "Well, another check from my flower shop."

I said, "Your flower shop?"

She said, "Yes, Elvis bought me a flower shop in California. I get a thousand dollars a week from them."

She put the envelope on a chair next to her and continued talking. Vernon walked outside and said, "Gladys, your hairdresser is here."

She said, "I will be back," and went into the house.

Elvis had two little dogs; they were as mean as could be. One of them jumped up and got the envelope off of the chair. That little dog took off running and shaking its head, with me chasing him all over the yard. I finally got the check away from the dog, with teeth marks in it. I took the check inside and told Gladys what happened. She said, "My gods, I left it outside; thank you, Lois." I went on back outside and Johnnie walked up and asked what was going on. He thought it was funny watching me chase that little dog.

In 1958, Elvis was drafted into the army.

Gladys was scared; all she could say was that the army was sending Elvis off to war. Her drinking grew more and more with Elvis now at Fort Hood, Texas. Gladys and Vernon joined Elvis, but would be forced to return to Memphis after Gladys became sick.

About six months after his induction into the army, Elvis received word that Gladys was very sick. He obtained an emergency leave and headed back to Memphis to be by her side.

THE DEATH OF GLADYS PRESLEY

ON AUGUST 13, 1958, JOHNNIE AND I WERE VISITING GLADYS IN THE hospital. We had been there all day, and Johnnie wouldn't stay in the room with us. I had been rubbing Gladys's feet and legs. They were very swollen and she was in a lot of pain. It was getting late and Johnnie was ready to go home. Gladys asked if I would spend the night with her; she didn't want to be alone tonight. I think she knew the end was near. I told Gladys if Johnnie would let me, I would stay. I went out into the hall where Johnnie was, and told him what Gladys had said, that she wanted me to stay the night with her. He said, "Lois, you know you can't stay. We have five kids at home. You need to take care of them." Johnnie could have watched the kids and allowed me to be with Gladys, but he wouldn't. I don't know if he didn't really understand just how bad Gladys was or if he just didn't care.

I went back in and told Gladys what Johnnie had said, and that he wouldn't let me stay.

You could see the tears and hurt in her eyes. I said, "Gladys, I'm sorry, but you know how he is, and I must go. I will be back in the morning. I love you."

She said, "I know you would stay if you could. I love you too."

I went back out to the hall and asked Johnnie one last time. I said, "Johnnie, that is your sister and she is dying. She will be all alone; please, let me stay with her."

He said, "Let's go, Lois."

All the way home, I didn't speak to him. When we got home, I told him, "You know she will not make it through the night."

He said, "She is not dying and she will be fine."

About 3:00 AM, a loud noise woke us up. It sounded like the door had slammed, but it couldn't have been the door; it was shut.

I told Johnnie that I think Gladys has just passed away. He said, "No she didn't. Go back to sleep."

I said, "Yes, I think she did, and she was here. You have made her mad, and she made that noise."

He said, "Go to sleep, Lois." He must have thought about what I said, because he couldn't sleep.

We stayed up the rest of the night. Later in the morning, we received word that Gladys had died. When Elvis arrived at the hospital, she had already passed away. He was torn apart by her death.

Elvis had Gladys brought back to Graceland for the services. The casket was placed in the Piano Room. Elvis stayed in his room much of the day; he finally came downstairs later in the evening. He walked into the living room and said, "Well, I gave her all she wanted and needed, except the thing she wanted most of all, were grandkids, and now it's too late."

Elvis placed a chair next to his mother's casket and looked at her for two days. Finally, Vernon came in and said, "Elvis, we must let her go." Elvis stood up and walked outside on the front steps and cried. Gladys was taken to the funeral home for the final services.

The Blackwood Brothers performed two gospel songs during the service. Gladys was taken to Forest Lawn to be laid to rest. At the end of the graveside services, Elvis jumped up and threw himself on his mother's casket, saying, "She's not dead, she's just sleeping."

Some of the guys had to pull Elvis off the casket. Now, I didn't see this, but have heard that Elvis carried his mother's nightgown with him all the time like a security blanket.

I have never seen a man act the way he did over his mother. Gladys's funeral was turned into a circus, and it hurt Elvis.

Money, fame, and life itself were nothing to Elvis without her. When Gladys Presley died, a large part of Elvis died with her.

THE LOVE OF MY LIFE

From "The Women Who Loved Elvis,"
Ladies' Home Journal, August 2007[*]

By Alanna Nash

On the thirtieth anniversary of Elvis's death, *Ladies' Home Journal* hunted down seven women who knew—and loved—Elvis.

THIRTY YEARS AFTER HIS DEATH, ON AUGUST 16, 1977, ELVIS Presley still holds sway—earning $42 million last year in marketing and product licensing, welcoming millions of visitors to Graceland, his Memphis home, and still popping up on the record charts now and then. But where the King of Rock and Roll proves most unforgettable is in the hearts of the women who loved and worked with him. Here, seven of them share their memories of the Elvis you never knew.

JUNE JUANICO, EARLY GIRLFRIEND

ELVIS WAS THE LOVE OF MY LIFE. I MET HIM IN THE SUMMER OF '55, when he was just a regional star. I was 17 and he was 20. He had

• • •

been in my hometown of Biloxi, Mississippi, several times before, and people said, "You need to see him," and I went on this one night. I thought he was the most gorgeous thing: big, dreamy eyes. Girls were screaming over him, and I'm just not that kind. I was passing by him, not even looking at him, and he reached through the crowd and grabbed my arm. He said, "Where are you going?"

What I remember most about that night was sitting in his car outside my house, just talking, while my mother kept an eye out to see what I was doing. The first thing I said was, "What is your real name?" I had never heard of a name like Elvis. And he said, "What do you mean my real name? My name is Elvis Aron Presley." We sat there until the sun came up at 6 A.M. He was shocked because my parents were divorced. He thought marriage was a lifelong thing, and when he got married, it was going to be forever. And he told me all about his twin who was dead at birth. I'd never met anybody quite like him.

We got so wrapped up in kissing on our very first date—nothing too sloppy, it was just marvelous—a little pecking here and there, a nibble here and there, then a serious bite.

But I didn't hear from him for a while after that. It turned out he was calling and my older brother wasn't bothering to tell me. Finally, he said, "Some guy with a hillbilly accent called."

For the one and a half years I dated him, our relationship remained chaste. He was just very tender and considerate. We spent so much time together, and we started talking about marriage. Mrs. Presley liked me. She saw me as domestic and wise for my young years. She was always telling me that Elvis needed someone to take care of him.

But Elvis was becoming more famous, and [manager] Colonel Tom Parker wanted him linked with actresses and Vegas showgirls.

Of course, Elvis liked legs that went on for days, and he brought one of those showgirls home for Christmas in '56. That did it for me. I decided to marry someone else. And Elvis said the Colonel said we couldn't get married, that he wouldn't dare do that to the Colonel.

The next time I saw him was in a movie theater in Memphis in the early '60s. I went down the row behind him and tapped him on the back, and he turned around and our eyes just locked. He got up and put me in a death grip. One of his guys ran over because he thought someone was abusing Elvis. But Elvis was holding on to me. Priscilla was sitting next to him, and she was very gracious. She kept her eyes glued to the screen.

In August 1977, my mother was at my house. I had laid down for a nap, and when I came out of my bedroom my mother was looking at me really strange. Finally, she said, "June!" She had tears in her eyes. She said, "I just heard on the television that Elvis Presley has died." I looked at her and said, "That can't be! That can't be!" I went over to the television and fell to my knees in front of it. I couldn't breathe. I honestly think if my mother had not been with me, I might have died. In my heart, I always thought Elvis and I would be together somewhere down the road. I was married for 36 years, and I've got two beautiful children and beautiful grandchildren. I've been blessed in many ways. But I have just never been able to stop loving Elvis.

WANDA JACKSON, ROCKABILLY PERFORMER

In July '55, I'd just graduated from high school. I already had a couple of hit songs in the country music field, and Bob Neal, the talent agent who also managed Elvis before Colonel Parker, said, "I'm booking a young man named Elvis Presley who is getting popular real fast, and we could use a girl on the show." I had no idea who he was. I met him at the radio station in Cape Girardeau, Missouri, that afternoon, and I was quite impressed—a real handsome guy. He was dressed a little flashier than the guys dressed back home in Oklahoma City—yellow coat, for example—and when he left the station I saw him get into a pink Cadillac. That was before the days of Mary Kay, and I had never seen a pink car before. We worked together that night. I was in my dressing room, and Elvis was going on, and all of a sudden my dad and I started hearing this screaming. My daddy said, "I wonder if there's a fire or something. Let me go look." I started getting my things, and he came back and said, "No, relax. But you've got to see this for yourself." He took me to the wings, and there was Elvis singing and moving and gyrating, and all these girls standing at the foot of the stage, screaming and reaching for him. It was quite an unusual sight for those days. And when the rest of the nation started giving him havoc, it really upset him. Mostly if they said anything too bad, he got mad, because in his mind he was having fun. I don't think he was trying to be vulgar. He was just being flirty with the girls.

We dated off and on for a little over a year on the tours. If we could get in a town early, and it was large enough to have a movie theater, we'd go to a matinee, and then after a show we'd go out to eat, usually with the other musicians and my daddy. Then sometimes we'd get a hamburger and just drive around the town and talk. We had a lot in common. He was a little older, and his career was beginning to blossom, and mine was, too. He was just a fine person. He loved to have fun and he laughed all the time. He didn't take himself seriously.

What was really sweet was the fact that he wanted to see me do good in my career. And he was just really eager that I try this kind of music like he was doing [rockabilly]. I'd say, "But Elvis, I'm just a country singer. I can't sing songs like that." He said, "You can, too. You've just gotta try."

In the early part of '56, he gave me one of his rings, a man's ring. It had little chipped diamonds. He wasn't very rich at that point. We were in Shreveport, Louisiana, and we'd done a matinee show, and he asked me if I'd step outside. We stood by his car, and he asked me if I'd be his girl. He'd just turned 21, and I was still 18. I had a crush on him, and being able to know him and know his heart made me admire him a lot. So I said I'd be his girl, and he gave me his ring. I wore it for about a year. Of course, this was before he met Priscilla. The last tour I worked with him was in January of '57, and after that he went to Hollywood to start his movie career. I think his head was just in a spin.

RAQUEL WELCH, ACTRESS

ROUSTABOUT IN 1964 WAS MY VERY FIRST FILM IN HOLLYWOOD. I WAS a bit player in the opening moments. Like many adolescents of the '50s, I had been completely gaga over Elvis. I saw him live in San Diego in one of his early shows. It was my first rock 'n' roll music concert ever. That was the first time that I ever conjured up what a sexy guy could be.

But when I saw him on the set of *Roustabout*, I was a little bit taken aback because something had changed about him. It seemed like he was more packaged. His clothes were not the same, his hair was obviously dyed now, and it was all sprayed into place. It was a little shocking to me because it was a whitewashed, cleaned-up Elvis. They took all the sex out of him!

He had these buddies, this group of guys that hung out with him, and you had to go through them to get to him. There was no such thing as walking up to Elvis on a set. At one point, one of his guys came over and said, "Elvis is having a little party at the house, and if you'd like to come up. . . ." And I thought, What? I wasn't sure if the invitation was from Elvis or from them, using Elvis. I had had a very strict upbringing, and I didn't like the setup, so I didn't go. I had a feeling that Elvis related so much more to men than women. I think he certainly liked women, but I just don't think he knew how to have a real relationship with one. He was a guy's guy.

Years later, about 1972, I had a contract to perform at the Las Vegas Hilton, and lo and behold, Elvis came in right after me. At his show he was dressed all in white, with bellbottoms with a little gold slit on the side, and a lot of jewelry and brocade coming down on his jacket and a high-neck collar. He looked almost like Liberace. I went to his dressing room, and he was very sweet, very nice, and he showed me all his jewelry. But he didn't seem to be really happy in his eyes.

MARY ANN MOBLEY, ACTRESS
AND MISS AMERICA 1959

ELVIS AND I FELT A COMMON BOND, COMING FROM MISSISSIPPI. HE thought I understood him. He didn't have to put on airs with me, and I wasn't after anything. This is an odd thing to say about Elvis Presley, but it was like I was working with my brother. We never dated. We were just two people from the same state. The first day I came on the set of *Girl Happy*, in 1964, Elvis stood up and said, "Where is Mary

Ann's chair?" All of a sudden a chair appeared with my name on it. That was the beginning of our friendship. I was 25 and he was 29. He and I would talk, and he asked me did I ever wonder about things that happened in my life. I said all the time. And he said, "Well, I do, too, especially about why I lived and my twin, Jessie Garon, didn't."

I think he put women in two categories. You were either one of the girls, or you were a lady. Once Priscilla had Lisa Marie in 1968, she became a Madonna figure for him. And I think that may be one reason why they split up. In Mississippi he was taught to be kind and take care of ladies, and then he had the other constantly thrown at him.

He used to say to me, "Mary Ann, one day I'm going to have a party I can invite you to." I took that as a compliment. And I never will forget, once one of the boys said "damn" in front of me, and Elvis said, "You never cuss in front of a lady."

Elvis would joke about the movies. When we were making *Harum Scarum*, he said, "This isn't going to change history, is it?" The sad thing is that Elvis was a better actor than the movies allowed him to be. He could have been great. I was told that much earlier, when Elvis was dating Natalie Wood, the director, Elia Kazan, offered him the lead opposite Natalie in *Splendor in the Grass*. And Colonel Tom refused.

Elvis invited my husband, Gary Collins, and me to come to Las Vegas for one of his openings in the '70s, and we went backstage. He was into the metaphysical, willing objects to move, that sort of thing. I was worried about it, but I thought, if that works for him. He was reading books, looking for answers.

People can say what they want about him shooting up TV sets, but I think he was depressed. And he was hooked on prescription drugs. It went on too long before anybody really knew he had a problem. He loved Southern food like I do. And he'd have to lose weight to get ready for the movies, and I think every doctor wanted to be Elvis' doctor, so no one said no to him about prescriptions. If one doctor said no, he'd find another one.

I wish that my husband and I had made more of an effort to seek him out as time went on. I think had there been someone to help him, he wouldn't have given up. I think he just got tired, and whatever kept him going before finally shut off. The medication that he was giving himself kicked in, and maybe he was tired of monitoring it, and just said, "Let whatever's going to happen happen."

JO SMITH, MARRIED TO ELVIS'
COUSIN BILLY SMITH

SOMETIMES ELVIS WAS LIKE THE DEVIL TO ME, BECAUSE I KNEW THE power he had over everybody who worked for him, including my husband. Billy was his first cousin, but he was more like his brother. Elvis couldn't live without Billy. Part of it was the connection to Elvis' mother, Gladys, I guess, because Billy was close to her. When he took him on trips, it was like he was taking him from me. When our first child was born, Elvis wouldn't let Billy come home. And I didn't understand that. When my second son was born, Elvis let Billy stay back for two days. Then I didn't see him again for three months.

This is a situation that all the wives of the guys who worked for Elvis went through. We threw rocks at the tour bus and wished them all dead. Elvis used to comment on how close Billy and I were. I think he wanted a similar lifestyle. But he wanted the closeness to be just on the wife's part. He never grew up. He didn't pay a lot of attention to Lisa. He didn't like to be bothered with children because he was too much of a child himself. And when she came to visit, somebody else watched her. He was protective, and he loved Lisa, but he had big things to do.

He loved you to talk babytalk to him, and we had to take care of him and cater to him like a small child. I did things I never thought I'd do—he liked to be put to bed and be told good night, the whole send-off. If you'd get up to leave the room, he'd say, "Where are you going? Come back here." He wanted you to stay until he fell asleep. Linda [Thompson] watched over him like a baby. She lotioned him and bathed him and gave him medicine.

I don't know how she did it. He was so strong in so many ways, and if you were with him, you felt safe. But in other ways, he was like a little kid. He was such a contradiction. He was very deep into his religion, from the way he was brought up. But as selfless as he was in religion, he always had to be number one in everything else. One time, everybody wanted to go bowling. So Elvis rented Bowlhaven Lanes, right down the street from Graceland. I don't guess he'd ever been bowling. Billy had been on a team, and several of the other guys had gone bowling in California, so they were pretty good. And Elvis wasn't good at all. He guttered, and he tried to throw the ball too hard. So that's the last time we ever went bowling. If he couldn't be the best at whatever we did, we didn't do it anymore.

LINDA THOMPSON, GIRLFRIEND

ELVIS WAS A VERY TENDER SOUL. HE HAD SUCH A GOOD HEART. WE literally bought out a pet shop one night. Elvis paid for about 20 dogs, just gave them out to his friends. And we kept this chow, little

Get-Low. He was a beautiful dog, but Elvis was going to get rid of him because we read an article that said chows turn on their masters 80 percent of the time. Elvis said, "I don't want to have to be worried about leaving this dog with you, or come home and find you have to have plastic surgery." But I said, "Oh, give the little fella a chance. He may turn out all right." So I raised him, and he turned out to be as gentle as a kitten. He was our sweetheart. But he had a congenital kidney ailment. I don't know if that made him so lethargic he didn't feel like being mean, but he had a wonderful disposition.

About three o'clock one morning, Get-Low was acting really strange, so we had a doctor come over. He said, "I don't think the dog will make it through the night." So Elvis leased a Learjet and flew Get-Low, my girlfriend and me, and the doctor up to Boston to a special clinic for kidney dialysis. We left him up there for about three months. But he didn't live long after that. He was only about a year old. We were on tour when he died, and we were coming home on his plane when they told us. Elvis just cried.

I was with him for four and a half years, from 1972 to 1976. He surrounded himself with people whom he loved and trusted, because he was so secluded from the world, and so sheltered. But a lot of people got very greedy. I think that's one reason Elvis felt lonely at times, he realized that even if they cared about him, they still lost sight of him as a human being. He would get depressed because he felt people didn't love him for being the simple person he was. They forgot about him as just a regular person with feelings like all of us.

I think it's a terrible thing for people to say they couldn't imagine Elvis growing old. Everybody has that right, even if they're a sex symbol. He wanted to live to be an old man. He wanted to see

Lisa have children, and he wanted to see his grandchildren. He had no idea he would die so young.

One morning at about seven we were lying in bed, and I felt something wasn't right. His breathing was strange. I shook him, and I said, "Honey, are you okay?" And he said, "I can't get my breath!" He had pneumonia. I called for the nurse, and she brought some oxygen over, and we had to rush him to the hospital. I stayed with him for two and a half weeks. Whenever he went to the hospital, I went to the hospital. So it was "we" went to the hospital.

Elvis needed more love and care than anybody I've ever met. Probably more than anybody in this world ever has. Because he was who he was, and what he was, and yet he had come from obscurity, from Tupelo, Mississippi, and poor parents. And he did enjoy having a mother image around him. But I think it's wonderful if you can be all things to each other. And he and I were. He called me "Mommy." And he was like my father at times. And we were like brother and sister at times, and we were like lovers at times. It was a full, rich relationship. For a long time, we didn't need anybody else, really. I truly, truly loved him, and I wouldn't have cared if he were John Doe. I loved him as a human soul. He was really a wonderful person. We often thought it would be fun to just go away and live in a little shack on a farm and just forget fame and fortune and all the craziness that goes with it.

KATHY WESTMORELAND, ELVIS' HIGH HARMONY SINGER AND FRIEND

EVERYBODY BLAMES THE COLONEL FOR WORKING ELVIS TOO HARD. But the Colonel got mixed signals from Elvis on how much to tour,

47

because Elvis would say, "I'm tired, I want to take some time off." And then at the same time he would say, "I'm home for two weeks and I'm bored. I have nothing to do." So the Colonel would go ahead and book shows, and then Elvis would end up tired. But then he'd say, "People have waited 20 years to see me, so I can't disappoint them." Or, "I have 300 people working for me. Their families depend on me working."

My last in-depth conversation with Elvis was just a few weeks before he died. I remember he said, "Kathy, what's it all about?" And I said, "I think that is for you to find out for yourself." He laughed and said, "That's the same answer I would have given you." And then he said, "People aren't going to remember me. I've never done anything lasting. I've never done a classic film. What can I do?" I said, "You've already done it. Just rest." He started talking about writing a book called *Through My Eyes*, and he talked about maybe producing.

At one of his last concerts, in Rapid City, South Dakota, there was a blue suit hanging on the wall that he was going to have to wear, and he was afraid he would look big in it. He said, "I'm going to look fat in that little suit, but I'll look good in my coffin." I didn't say anything because I knew that it was inevitable and could happen at any moment.

YOU'LL BE NEXT
ON MY LIST

From Declassified FBI memo dated 2-20-1964

"Presdient" Elvis Presley tops an impressive list on a postcard from a potential assassin.

FD-36 (Rev. 12-13-56)

FBI

Date: **2/20/64**

Transmit the following in _____
(Type in plain text or code)

Via _____**AIRTEL**_____
(Priority or Method of Mailing)

TO: DIRECTOR, FBI

FROM: SAC, MEMPHIS (9-1231) (C)

UNSUB, AKA ▓▓▓▓▓▓▓▓▓▓▓▓▓
ELVIS PRESLEY - VICTIM
EXTORTION; POSSIBLE THREAT TO PRESIDENT
OF UNITED STATES

Re Bureau Airtel to Memphis, 2/19/64.

There is enclosed original of post card postmarked
Huntsville, Ala., Jan. 10, 1964, 5:30 PM, bearing handwritten
address, "Presdient Elvis Presly   Memphis S, tennessee," and
bearing on the reverse side handwritten note, "You will be
nest on my list...."

The enclosed post card was forwarded to the Bureau
with Memphis Airtel 1/15/64, captioned as above, and was
returned to Memphis by the FBI Laboratory by Laboratory Report
dated 1/20/64. The enclosure is for referral to U. S. Secret
Service, Washington, D. C.

③ - Bureau (Enc.-1) (RM)
1 - Memphis
COH:ME
(4)

REC-123

Approved: _____ Sent _____ M Per _____
Special Agent in Charge

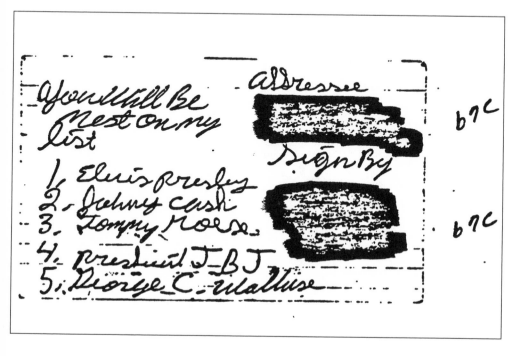

TURNED LOOSE AGAIN

From *Elvis Presley*, "The Comeback Special"[*]

By Bobbie Ann Mason

The novelist, short story writer, essayist, and author of *In Country* wrote a biography of Elvis Presley for the Penguin Lives series. This excerpt creates a vivid snapshot of Elvis in the mid to late sixties.

EVEN THE COLONEL KNEW IT WAS TIME FOR A CHANGE. WITH movie profits plummeting and Elvis's interest in making the movies ever dwindling, something had to happen. *Speedway* barely recovered production costs. Record sales were also still in decline.

Many of the fans were begging him to give up the movies and tour again. Elvis needed some fresh music. The same thing had happened with his recordings as with the movies—he got lousy material. The singer-songwriter trend dominated now, and artists such as John Lennon and Paul McCartney wanted to keep the full rights to their own songs when other musicians recorded them. But the Colonel

• • •

had always demanded a share of the songwriter's royalties as well as a share in the publishing rights to the songs Elvis recorded. His deal with Hill and Range Publishers limited Elvis's choices of songs to the material it gathered. So Elvis had little chance of recording anything from outside that stable.

Elvis, with no impulse to write his own music, loved singing and interpreting songs his own way. He loved the thrill of harmonizing with other voices, especially on gospel songs. But his efforts often seemed to be sabotaged. Again and again, after he had worked on a song to perfection, record company technicians mixed the song differently, so that what he heard on the release was different from what he had endorsed in the studio. This loss of artistic control angered him. He knew the Colonel was meddling, and he felt helpless.

But when he recorded "Big Boss Man" and "Guitar Man," an upbeat Jerry Reed song, in late 1967, his spirits rose. Although the single of "Big Boss Man" reached only number thirty-eight on the charts, the recording session, in Nashville, had stirred Elvis as nothing in the studio had in a long while. After a long period of lethargy and dissatisfaction with cranking out soundtrack albums, Elvis seemed to find the spark he needed to pull out of his funk. He realized it was now or never—get moving again or sink into oblivion. The Nashville session reignited his hopes of making good music.

Before long, Elvis was able to leave Hollywood, to walk away from the brain-rotting movies. The opportunity arose in 1968, when NBC proposed a TV special. For the first time in seven years, Elvis was going to perform onstage before an audience. The young producer, Steve Binder, was intent on resurrecting the lost Elvis, and he had a specific vision for the show: a stripping away of the movie-star Elvis and a return to the Elvis who had revolutionized popular music—the original rebel rocker, with the dark, threatening image. Although the Colonel envisioned the show as a tame Christmas special with songs like "The Little Drummer Boy" and "Santa Claus Is Coming to Town," Binder had no intention of letting this unique chance for Elvis to do his real stuff be smothered by a sentimental formula.

As Elvis immersed himself in the project, the Colonel stewed on the sidelines, but he didn't interfere this time. He knew they had to go in a new direction; the movie formula no longer worked. As he did in 1956, the Colonel turned to TV for exposure. For Elvis, the TV special was a daring move, occurring so soon after the Beatles' *Sgt. Pepper's Lonely Hearts Club Band* had redefined popular music by blurring the boundary between low art and high art. The Beatles, almost playfully, had challenged popular art to grow and had challenged highbrow audiences to pay attention to lowbrow possibility. Elvis made his bravest decision of the decade. He jumped up and reclaimed his title.

The show followed a story line, the journey of the "Guitar Man" through success, corruption and salvation. The thematic structure was based on a classic story, *The Blue Bird*, by the Belgian playwright Maurice Maeterlinck. The show consisted of several production members alternating with songs from an informal jam session that had been filmed separately before a studio audience. The jam session was the best part of the show. For that, Elvis had recruited his original musicians, Scotty Moore and drummer D. J. Fontana. (Bill Black had died.) Elvis's form-fitting black leather suit was an unforgettable costume, the essence of Elvis the rocker. With his wicked black hair, Elvis appeared as lithe and smooth and sensuous as a panther. Having lost weight, he was lean and beautiful—he had never looked better.

Elvis himself was terrified, fearing failure. He worried most about the informal talking he was supposed to do during the jam session—telling stories without a script. He had progressed far beyond the tendency to mumble, but he was still shy about speaking up. "What if nobody likes me?" Elvis kept asking. He almost backed out at the last minute, but he met the challenge, drawing on his self-effacing charm to hide his fear. He was filmed sitting in a sort of boxing ring, laughing and bantering with Scotty and D. J. and a couple of others. You could still see the deference, the down-look. Elvis played with his image. He laughed at it. His modesty was seductive, winning. He made fun of his trademark lip curl. He sang a ballad, "Are You Lonesome Tonight?," and fooled around with a mock Ink Spots–style recitation. The banter and camaraderie, however nervous Elvis was, weren't stilted or programmed, but natural and real.

Standing in the leather suit in the small arena, he performed a medley of his hits: a fierce "Heartbreak Hotel," "Hound Dog," "All Shook Up." He sang with stunning control and energy. All his talent—suppressed so long during his Hollywood years—came surging back, full force. He was a revelation. Long-legged, with long-toed motorcycle boots, he stood in that rocking posture of the laborer, legs forming an arch, as if he were ready to swing an ax to fell an oak. He performed old songs like "Lawdy Miss Clawdy" and "That's All Right (Mama)" while sitting down, his heebie-jeebie legs still working. But now he seemed sleek, sophisticated, polished, his raw urgency under control. In part, it was illusion—Elvis the pro, putting on his Elvis act. But in part, what the audience saw was the truth—Elvis returning to his true vocation, reveling in it, and reclaiming a more deeply felt sense of himself. In any event, it was mesmerizing. Elvis's energy, masked by his recent dreadful movies, burst forth. He seemed grown now, sexually provocative in an adult way. The sixties may have meant the sexual revolution, with rock music exploding and exploring sexual freedom, but none of the rock groups of the sixties exuded sensuality as Elvis did in this 1968 show. One doesn't recall the Jefferson Airplane, Herman's Hermits, Janis Joplin, the Grateful Dead, or even the Beatles as being especially sexy. For all the raunchiness of the Rolling Stones, Mick Jagger's moves were so peculiar that Elvis found him hilarious. Certainly Mick was no Adonis.

During rehearsals for the special, Billy Goldenberg, the arranger, was surprised to find Elvis one day picking out Beethoven's *Moonlight Sonata* on the piano. The two began working on it together every night, enjoying the quiet diversion into a rich, sophisticated music. Then one night two or three of Elvis's guys interrupted them and spoiled the mood with a snide putdown of classical music. Goldenberg said that Elvis immediately stopped playing, "as if some strange, dark shadow had come over the place." Elvis was embarrassed that his guys had seen him flirting with high-tone, uptown art—art that violated their shared tastes. The Beatles had crossed that line, but Elvis was still afraid of being laughed at if he jumped into an unfamiliar highbrow domain.

The show was taped in the summer of 1968, and Martin Luther King had been killed in Memphis. Elvis, who was deeply affected by what had happened in his own town, realized that it was time to abandon frivolous songs and sing what he believed and felt. The closing number of the show, "If I Can Dream," was written for Elvis specifically to express his dreams of freedom and equality. The song seemed to echo King's famous "I Have a Dream" speech.

The show, which became known informally as "The Comeback Special," aired on NBC in December 1968, and was a huge surprise success—as if the Elvis of 1956 had been turned loose again. But the changing times made him seem less of an anomaly at this later date. In the midst of war, social turmoil, and assassinations, Elvis was a welcome old friend, not an assault on decency. The *New York Times* changed its tune from "vulgar" (1956) to "charismatic." The single "If I Can Dream" became Elvis's biggest hit in years.

Early in 1969, genuinely invigorated by making good music again, Elvis went into American Studio in Memphis, which had become the center of soul music. There, back on his home turf, he was challenged musically more than he had been at any time since Sam Phillips invited him into Sun Studio. At American, with studio head Chips Moman and with the producer from Nashville, Felton Jarvis, Elvis recorded some of his best music of the decade— "Suspicious Minds," "Long Black Limousine," "Kentucky Rain," "I Can't Stop Loving You," and numerous others. He brought a new depth of feeling and a heightened artistry to these innovative new recordings. He had never worked with such enthusiasm. The songs from the American sessions captured the new musical directions Elvis had been thinking about for some time, incorporating elements of contemporary country, gospel, soul, and blues into his style. He immersed himself in the new songs with a passion and depth that he hadn't expressed since he recorded his spiritual album *How Great Thou Art* in 1966. Elvis the artist emerged again with confidence in his musical instincts. Although he hesitated at first, he even risked doing a kind of song he had usually avoided—a song with a political overtone. "If I Can Dream" had paved the way for "In the Ghetto," a socially aware song more suited to the times than what Elvis had been recording. [Music critic] Peter Guralnick calls "In the Ghetto," "Suspicious Minds," and "Only the Strong Survive" "a new hybrid style, a cross between 'Old Shep' and contemporary soul, in which Elvis can fully believe." This was the direction Elvis wanted, songs he could pour his heart into, songs that would let him use his voice sincerely and completely. Now he could give full reign to the sounds from his accumulated experience, going back to earliest childhood—the desolate moans, as well as shouts of celebration and exuberance, that came from the downtrodden people around him. Even if Elvis didn't remember what he heard at Parchman Farm, or even if his father never repeated the chants, he did hear sounds of the blues everywhere around him. He grew up in Mississippi, after all. Elvis would have heard sundown field hollers—the long-drawn-out moans of liberation at the end of the workday—right in East Tupelo. The sounds would have carried from the nearby fields around, and from the neighborhood of Shake Rag. The sounds of the blues—levee-camp moans, juke-joint blues, work chants—were in the air. Elvis absorbed them deep into his soul. The sounds he sang at the end of the sixties came out of his own life—the fight against poverty, the struggle to become somebody, the humiliations suffered by the country person, the loss of his mother, the shame of his father's Parchman sentence. One of the songs Elvis recorded in the Memphis sessions was "I Washed My Hands in Muddy Water," a poignant, personal story-song about the sins of the father visited upon the son—a story about crime and prison. But the public did not know how personal this was.

Elvis knew he wanted to perform live again. At the conclusion of the taping of the TV special back in the summer, he had told the Colonel he wanted to tour again. The Colonel was making plans. Now, after slogging through his final movie commitment, *Change of Habit*, Elvis was ready.

MR. PRESIDENT, THIS IS MR. ELVIS PRESLEY

From *The Day Elvis Met Nixon*[*]

By Egil "Bud" Krogh

We've all seen the famous photograph of President Richard Nixon shaking hands with Elvis Presley inside the Oval Office. Now, here's the story behind the famous image from a former Nixon White House aide.

12:30 PM

ELVIS AND I WALKED THROUGH THE ROOSEVELT ROOM AND across the hall to the northwest door to the Oval Office. A Secret Service agent, who was stationed there when the President was in the office, greeted us. He opened the door and I ushered Elvis in.

Entering the Oval Office for the first time to meet the President can be a rather intimidating experience for almost anyone. My first

• • •

visit to brief the President sure had intimidated me. That meeting had taken place in January of 1969, a couple days after the Inauguration. I was asked to brief the President on the government's proposed policy for dealing with anti-war demonstrations and protests. The issue was under the jurisdiction of the Counsel to the President, John Ehrlichman, and he had assigned specific responsibility to me.

I remember entering the Oval Office and seeing the President reclining in his chair behind his desk with his feet crossed on the desktop. Because I was just a staff person joining an informal meeting already in progress with Ehrlichman, there wasn't any reason for the President to get up. I took a chair directly in front of the desk, and found myself staring at the soles of the President's shoes. His face was totally blocked out.

During that first visit of mine, I remember Ehrlichman saying, "Mr. President, Bud Krogh here has been responsible for developing our policy on protests here in D.C. Let him give you a rundown on what we're doing."

The President then simply widened the split between his crossed shoes, and I found myself staring into his face framed by the "V" of his soles. For a split second, all my cognitive and communicative functions ceased. The President of the United States was looking at *me* for information. Fortunately, I had taken the precaution of writing down on a yellow pad the leading points I wanted to make. After glancing down at them, I was able to get a few words out, which enabled me to get rolling on the briefing. The initial panic, however, had been real.

While Elvis' reaction on entering the Oval Office wasn't exactly panic, it nevertheless wasn't what I had expected. He was one of the most famous individuals in the world, someone who had entertained millions of people. I expected him to be immediately at ease on entering the Oval Office. Such was not the case.

He walked in a step in front of me and stopped. He looked up at the ceiling, which had a large eagle emblazoned in the plaster. He looked down at the blue carpeting on the floor which had another eagle centered in the Presidential seal. Eagles adorned the tops of the armed service flags to the right of the President's desk. The Presidential seal that had been embroidered by Julie Eisenhower during the 1968 campaign and given to him in the early hours right after he had "gone over the top" to win the election was hanging on the wall just to the right of the door Elvis entered. I noticed Elvis observe everything and then hesitantly walk forward to greet the President. He seemed to be awed if not overwhelmed by it all.

President Nixon got up from his chair as we entered the room and walked around his desk to meet Elvis. He was wearing a gray suit with the American flag in his lapel. Ollie Atkins, the White House photographer, began taking pictures as soon as they reached each other. Because the meeting was to be brief, known in White House parlance as a "drop-by," there was no plan to sit down in the couches, which faced each other in front of the fireplace or in the chairs on either side of the President's desk.

As they started to shake hands, I said, "Mr. President, this is Mr. Elvis Presley." Elvis was still wearing his sunglasses and holding the badges and pictures in his left hand.

They continued shaking hands for a few seconds while Ollie Atkins snapped their picture. The President then started the conversation: "It's very good to meet you, Mr. Presley. I appreciate your offer to help us on the drug problem." While to the world, Elvis Presley was thought of simply as Elvis, in the very formal White House of 1970, he was addressed as Mr. Presley. Elvis didn't respond to the President's greeting, but just kept smiling. So I jumped in. "Mr. President, Mr. Presley has told me that he can reach a lot of young people through his music to help them stay off or get off drugs." I tried to get the conversation underway by mentioning something Elvis earlier had told me he wanted to say.

After a few awkward seconds, Elvis said: "Mr. President, thank you for seeing me. I'd like to show you some pictures of my family and some of my badges." After saying this, he stepped over to the President's desk and spread out his badges and pictures. The President stood next to him.

Elvis selected first the picture of Priscilla and himself and handed it to the President. The President picked it up and smiled. Elvis then said, "And here's a picture of my daughter, Lisa Marie," as he handed her picture to the President. Elvis seemed to be getting over his initial shyness.

"She's a beautiful little girl," the President said. Elvis smiled.

Elvis then picked up various police badges and started showing them to the President. "I have a collection of badges from police departments around the country," he said. "I really support what our police have to do." The President responded: "They certainly deserve all the support we can give them. They've got tough jobs."

The President then said: "Mr. Presley, let's let Ollie take some pictures over here." The President then directed Elvis to a position in front of the military service flags, and Ollie Atkins took a number of pictures of them there. This position in the Oval Office was a popular place for taking pictures of the President and his guests.

They stepped back to the desk where Elvis pulled up his sleeve to show him his cuff links. The President bent over Elvis' right arm to get a good look at the cuff link. I was standing several feet away observing this and taking down notes of what they said.

Elvis continued by saying, "I've been performing a lot in Las Vegas. Quite a place." The President responded with a smile. "I know very well how difficult it is to play Las Vegas," he said. I don't know what campaign visit the President was alluding to or what he had heard from his friends in the entertainment industry that prompted this comment.

The President continued: "As Bud mentioned, Mr. Presley, I think you can reach young people in a way no one in the government can. It's important that you keep your credibility." It seemed that the President was becoming concerned that the visit remain confidential so that Elvis' credibility, and perhaps his own, would not be impaired.

Elvis answered: "I do my thing just by singing, Mr. President. I don't make any speeches on stage. I just try to reach them in my own way." The President nodded his agreement to this.

The conversation then took an odd turn. Elvis said: "The Beatles, I think, are kind of anti-American. They came over here. Made a lot of money. And then went back to England. And they said some anti-American stuff when they got back."

I didn't have a clue what Elvis was referring to. He hadn't brought up the Beatles at all in our earlier meeting. From the look of surprise on the President's face when Elvis said this, I was convinced the President didn't know what he was talking about either. Maybe there was an element of jealousy in Presley's comment, as by the time of the meeting with the President, the Beatles were the hottest rock group in the world and had eclipsed Elvis in popularity for some younger fans.

The President then said: "You know, those who use the drugs

are the protesters. You know, the ones who get caught up in dissent and violence. They're the same group of young people."

"Mr. President," Elvis said, "I'm on your side. I want to be helpful. And I want to help get people to respect the flag because that's getting lost."

The flag was also a new topic. I wasn't sure what precipitated this comment. Maybe it was the American flag in the President's lapel, or the armed services flags, or the stories of flag burning which Elvis probably had heard. Whatever the cause, it was clear Elvis was trying to find things to say that the President would approve of.

"I'm just a poor boy from Tennessee. I've gotten a lot from my country. And I'd like to do something to repay for what I've gotten."

"That will be very helpful," the President replied. "We need a lot of help on this drug problem."

Elvis continued: "I've been studying Communist brainwashing for over ten years now, and the drug culture, too."

The last comment took us into uncharted waters. I could see the President was having a hard time, as was I, in following the linkage between Communist brainwashing and the drug culture. I thought it would be prudent to bring the conversation back to a safer harbor.

"Mr. President," I said, "Mr. Presley told me that he's accepted by many of those we'd like to reach with our anti-drug message."

The President nodded again, and Elvis said: "I can go right into a group of hippies and young people and be accepted. This can be real helpful."

The President paused before replying: "Well, that's fine. But just be sure you don't lose your credibility."

Elvis then asked a question that caught me by surprise.

"Mr. President, can you get me a badge from the Narcotics

Bureau? I've been trying to get a badge from them for my collection." He pointed again to some of the police badges he had put on the President's desk. In the earlier meeting in my office, Elvis had told me about his support for police and law enforcement departments around the country. He said he liked to drop in on police departments by surprise, and give a gift of cash or some other expensive item. The police would then often give him a badge in return. While he had mentioned he wanted "some kind of credential," he hadn't specified a badge from the Bureau of Narcotics and Dangerous Drugs.

The President looked a little uncertain at this request. He turned to me and asked, "Bud, can we get him a badge?"

I couldn't read what the President really wanted me to say.

"Well, sir," I answered, "If you want to give him a badge, I think we can get him one."

The President nodded. "I'd like to do that. See that he gets one."

"Yes, sir," I responded.

Elvis was smiling triumphantly. "Thank you very much, sir. This means a lot to me." He seemed to be energized if not overcome by this. "Mr. President, I really do support what you're doing, and I want to help."

Elvis then moved up close to the President and, in a spontaneous gesture, put his left arm around him and hugged him. President hugging was not, at least in my limited experience, a common occurrence in the Oval Office. It caught the President—and me—off guard. The President recovered from his surprise and patted Elvis on the shoulder. "Well, I appreciate your willingness to help us out, Mr. Presley."

Elvis then went back to the desk. "I'd like you to have these pictures. And I also brought a gift for you, a real fine collector's World War II Colt .45. The Secret Service guy received it for you."

"Thank you very much," the President said. "That's very kind of you."

Elvis then scooped up his badges and turned to go. He looked like a kid who had just received all of the Christmas presents he'd asked for. He turned back to the President.

"Mr. President, would you have a little time just to say hello to my two friends, Sonny West and Jerry Schilling? It would mean a lot to them and to me."

The President looked at me. "Bud, do we have time for that?" The President knew that during Open Hour visitors get stacked up pretty tightly.

"Yes, sir," I said, flying blindly. "I think we have a few more minutes." I thought that Sonny and Jerry would enjoy meeting the President and it seemed a shame to spoil the ebullient mood. "I'll go get them."

I walked over to the door and asked the agent to bring Sonny and Jerry to the Oval Office. When they walked in, they both looked delighted and a little dazed. As we came over to the desk, the President shook hands with them both. I had asked that Ollie Atkins return to the office. He took pictures of Elvis, Sonny and Jerry with the President.

The President said, as he was shaking hands, "You've got a couple of big ones here, Elvis."

"They're good friends, Mr. President. And they are interested in helping you out, too."

"I appreciate what you're all doing," the President said. "As I said before, just be sure you keep your credibility." He then walked around to the front of his desk and opened the bottom left hand drawer. In this drawer the President kept gifts he could give to his visitors.

"Let's see here," said the President. "Here are some tie clasps." The tie clasps had the Presidential seal on them, and while they were probably great gifts for most men, I wasn't sure Elvis, Sonny or Jerry even owned any ties. Elvis, obviously curious about what else was in the drawer, walked over behind the desk. He and the President started rummaging through the drawer together.

"Remember, Mr. President, they've got wives," Elvis said, picking up some pins with the Presidential seal on them. Golf balls, cuff links, and pins were laid on the desk. I'm not sure which gifts were finally given, but after the raid on the drawer, Elvis, Sonny and Jerry had their hands full. They all seemed delighted with what they had received.

The President then escorted them to the door. "Thank you very much, fellas," he said.

Elvis, Sonny and Jerry all thanked the President, shook hands, and I guided them into the hall by the Secret Service agent's desk. The agent got up and closed the door.

It was 1:05 PM.

A SOBER,
CLEAN-MINDED
YOUNG MAN

From Declassified FBI memo dated 1-4-1971

After his visit to see Richard Nixon, Elvis sought an audience with J. Edgar Hoover at FBI headquarters. Although he didn't meet with Hoover, he did get a tour.

UNITED STATES GOVERNMENT

Memorandum

: — Mr. Bishop   DATE: 12-30-70

FROM :   M. A. Jones

SUBJECT :   WILLIAM N. MORRIS
FORMER SHERIFF, SHELBY COUNTY, TENNESSEE
ELVIS PRESLEY
REQUEST FOR BUREAU TOUR AND MEET WITH
THE DIRECTOR

      Mr. William N. Morris, former Sheriff, Shelby County, Memphis, Tennessee, telephoned Assistant Director Casper from the Washington Hotel today and advised that he was in town with the well-known entertainer Elvis Presley and six other people in Presley's party and inquired concerning the possibility of a tour of our facilities and an opportunity to meet and shake hands with the Director tomorrow, 12-31-70. Morris indicated to Mr. Casper that Presley had just received an award from the President for his work in discouraging the use of narcotics among young people and for his assistance in connection with other youth problems in the Beverly Hills, California, area.

      Mr. Casper advised Morris that the Director was out of the city, however, that he, Casper, would see what could be done to arrange a tour for Morris, Presley and party. Morris advised that he could be reached at Room 702, Washington Hotel, telephone number 638-5900.

BACKGROUND:

      By memorandum dated 12-22-70, which is attached, you will recall that Senator George Murphy (Republican-California) telephoned your office on 12-21-70 and advised that Presley had accompanied him, Murphy, to Washington on a flight from Los Angeles and expressed interest in meeting the Director during his stay in Washington.

      Murphy described Presley as a very sincere young man who was interested in becoming active in the drive against the use of narcotics, particularly by young people. Murphy indicated that he had arranged an appointment for Presley with John Ingersoll, Director of the Bureau of Narcotics and Dangerous Drugs.

      Murphy was advised that the Director was out of the city and not expected to return until around the first of the year at which point he requested that someone from the Bureau get in touch with Presley and express the Director's regrets. This was done.

Enclosures (2)

1 - Mr. Sullivan	1 - Mr. Casper	1 - Miss Holmes	1 - Tour Room
1 - Mr. Bishop	1 - Miss Gandy	1 - Mr. Malmfeldt	1 - M. A. Jones
1 - Mr. Mohr			

GTQ:cl (10)   CONTINUED - OVER

M. A. Jones to Mr. Bishop Memo
RE: WILLIAM N. MORRIS AND ELVIS PRESLEY

INFORMATION IN BUFILES:

Bufiles reflect that Presley has been the victim in a number of extortion attempts which have been referred to the Bureau. Our files also reflect that he is presently involved in a paternity suit pending in Los Angeles, California, and that during the height of his popularity during the latter part of the 1950's and early 1960's his gyrations while performing were the subject of considerable criticism by the public and comment in the press. The files of the Identification Division fail to reflect any arrest record for Presley.

Our Memphis Office advised that relations with former Sheriff Morris were excellent during the period he was in office, and that several men from his department were accepted for attendance at the FBI National Academy while he was Sheriff. According to Memphis, Morris is now associated with a public relations firm in that city, but that he has political ambitions and it is anticipated that he will eventually run for Mayor of Memphis.

Our files and the files of the Director's Office fail to reflect that the Director has ever met Presley or Morris.

OBSERVATIONS:

Presley's sincerity and good intentions notwithstanding he is certainly not the type of individual whom the Director would wish to meet. It is noted at the present time he is wearing his hair down to his shoulders and indulges in the wearing of all sorts of exotic dress. A photograph of Presley clipped from today's "Washington Post" is attached and indicates Presley's personal appearance and manner of dress.

RECOMMENDATION:

That the Director permit someone from your office to return former Sheriff Morris' call and advise him that while we will be pleased to afford him, Presley and their party a special tour of our facilities tomorrow, 12-31-70, that it will not be possible for the Director to see them.

-2-

M. A. Jones to Bishop Memo
RE: ELVIS PRESLEY

competent to address large groups but much rather prefers small gatherings in community centers and the like, where he makes himself accessible for talks and discussions regarding the evils of narcotics and other problems of concern to teenagers and other young people.

Following their tour, Presley privately advised that he has volunteered his services to the President in connection with the narcotics problem and that Mr. Nixon had responded by furnishing him an Agent's badge of the Bureau of Narcotics and Dangerous Drugs. Presley was carrying this badge in his pocket and displayed it.

Presley advised that he wished the Director to be aware that he, Presley, from time to time is approached by individuals and groups in and outside of the entertainment business whose motives and goals he is convinced are not in the best interests of this country and who seek to have him to lend his name to their questionable activities. In this regard, he volunteered to make such information available to the Bureau on a confidential basis whenever it came to his attention. He further indicated that he wanted the Director to know that should the Bureau ever have any need of his services in any way that he would be delighted to be of assistance.

Presley indicated that he is of the opinion that the Beatles laid the groundwork for many of the problems we are having with young people by their filthy unkempt appearances and suggestive music while entertaining in this country during the early and middle 1960's. He advised that the Smothers Brothers, Jane Fonda, and other persons in the entertainment industry of their ilk have a lot to answer for in the hereafter for the way they have poisoned young minds by disparaging the United States in their public statements and unsavory activities.

Presley advised that he resides at 3764 Highway 51, South, Memphis, Tennessee, but that he spends a substantial portion of his time in the Beverly Hills, California - Las Vegas, Nevada, areas fulfilling motion picture assignments and singing commitments.

He noted that he can be contacted anytime through his Memphis address and that because of problems he has had with people tampering with his mail, such correspondence should be addressed to him under the pseudonym Colonel Jon Burrows.

- 2 -

CONTINUED - OVER

M. A. Jones to Bishop Memo
RE: ELVIS PRESLEY

It should be here noted following their tour and prior to their departure from the building, Mr. Morris indicated that Presley had been recently selected by the Junior Chamber of Commerce as one of the "ten outstanding men" in the United States and that of these ten in a ceremony to be held in Memphis sometime in January, 1971, Presley would be named as the "most outstanding" of the ten. According to Morris, similar recognition was afforded President Nixon some 25 years ago and the late President Kennedy was also a recipient of this award.

Morris observed that he has known Presley for many years, that despite his manner of dress, he is a sober, clean minded young man who is good to his family and his friends and who is very well regarded by all, including the law enforcement community in the Memphis Tennessee, area where he was raised and still resides.

Presley, Morris, and their party expressed appreciation for the courtesies extended them.

OBSERVATION:

Presley did give the impression of being a sincere, young man who is conscious of the many problems confronting this country. In view of his unique position in the entertainment business, his favorable comments concerning the Director and the Bureau, and his offer to be of assistance as well as the fact that he has been recognized by the Junior Chamber of Commerce and the President, it is felt that a letter from the Director would be in order.

RECOMMENDATION:

That the attached letter to Presley be approved and sent.

- 3 -

HE DIDN'T
EVEN SEEM REAL

From *Breathing Out*, chapters 43 and 44[*]

By Peggy Lipton with David and Coco Dalton

The fashion icon and star of the hit TV series *The Mod Squad* describes her short romance with Elvis in 1971.

THE KING AND I

IT WAS 1971, RIGHT IN THE MIDDLE OF MY RAPACIOUSLY ROMANTIC period, that I met Elvis Presley. I ended up spending three long weekends with him. Two in Lake Tahoe and one in Las Vegas. People who heard about my fling with him assumed I must have met him at some Hollywood gathering. But you couldn't really meet Elvis socially because Elvis lived in his own bubble and he never left it. He was a rock-and-roll hermit who surrounded himself with people who adjusted their lives to his reality. To meet him you had to enter his bubble.

• • •

I had two very smart girlfriends (Janet and Shelly) who were both actresses and seeing Elvis at the time. I would listen to their stories about him. I was fascinated by what they told me and became mildly curious. Janet insisted that I meet him. I really didn't understand why. It seemed to bode trouble somehow—how could I possibly have anything in common with Elvis Presley?

"I've been talking to Elvis about you, and I really want you to come to Lake Tahoe to meet him," Janet insisted. Later on, of course, she wanted to kill me. But what did she expect?

Both of these girls were crazy about Elvis; they were also my very good friends. Shelly had had the longer affair with him and then moved on to the next thing. They adored Elvis but they also agreed he was a piece of work—by which they meant that fragile, outsized, damaged ego of his. Still, despite all his problems and weirdness, everyone fell in love with him.

Of course, I was intrigued by the idea of meeting him—this was Elvis, after all, the sacred monster of rock 'n' roll, but still I resisted. Finally at Janet's insistence, I gave my phone number over and in doing so a short, strange destiny unfolded for Elvis and me. Joe Esposito, Elvis's right-hand man, called me frequently. At first I wouldn't take the calls. Not playing hard to get, just sensing that for me it would be one more disaster.

"Elvis would like to talk to you," Joe said when I finally picked up. A moment later, Elvis got on the phone. His voice affected me right away. It was deep and glue-like—with a thick Tennessee drawl that had a built-in echo. He talked the way he sang. I heard his words as if he were in the middle of a song. An *Elvis* song, for God's sake. I had no choice. Think about it. The next thing I knew, he'd invited me to come to Tahoe, and I had said yes.

Elvis had his people call me to say he would be sending a car to take me to the airport. I took a little overnight bag. I was a kid. Maybe not sexually innocent, but still young. I was going to spend a weekend with the supposedly sexiest, most sensual celebrity of my time. My ego, curiosity, and need for conquest was taking over—as it inevitably did.

Still, I felt unnerved and frightened. I was afraid he was going to overwhelm me. I was already overwhelmed by the mere *notion* of Elvis. Like millions of others when we were growing up, I had idolized him. His persona was phantasmagorical; he didn't even seem real. But soon Elvis would become more real than I could possibly have imagined.

THE EMPEROR'S NEW CLOTHES

WHEN I WAS NINE YEARS OLD, MY BEST FRIEND, PENNY, AND I HAD danced in her bedroom in Lawrence, N.Y., to "Don't Be Cruel" over and over—trying to divine the essence of this sexual, gyrating being and summon him into ours. All very natural, very normal.

When I saw his plane sitting on the runway, I wasn't sure how "natural and normal" any of this was. Climbing up the steps, I was excited, queasy, and apprehensive.

Suddenly, I was on the plane. And there he was, sitting in the cabin in full white regalia complete with sunglasses, rings, and tows of gold chains. Not exactly what you would call casual. Elvis looked like an action figure of himself. The clash of our lifestyles hit me like a ton of bricks. I suddenly felt embarrassed and panicky. I wanted to get off the plane immediately. It didn't feel quite as claustrophobic as the boat in the Bahamas with Sammy Davis, but it was still upsetting. When he looked into my eyes, he suddenly became shy and I liked that.

I had dressed for the occasion. A slinky T-shirt, tight bell bottoms, and boots. And, oh yeah, I was already a TV star and supposedly being pursued by multitudes of fans—I had it all going on, baby. But somewhere gnawing at me was the image of the stammering pimply faced girl from the Five Towns. On some subtle level I was meeting my match. In my own way, I was putting up as much of a front as he was. We both seemed to be reveling in the fanfare of a Venetian masquerade. At that point, however, he had pursued and had won the first rally of the game.

"Hello, darlin'," he said. His voice was sexy and inviting—and spookily familiar. His eyes danced. He was sitting at a small table and it was from there that, like some oriental potentate, he offered me jewelry. I said no thank you to the blue suede cases he opened and offered as gifts to me, even before the plane left the tarmac. His gesture was so immediate I knew he had offered similar tokens before to others. Was it a way of bonding, or gaining some control over the situation? I didn't care. It was probably his way of saying welcome to my world. In the end, I said okay to one square ring with tiny diamonds, rubies, and sapphires that you could move around to form any letter. When he handed it to me I saw it was a "P." For Presley or Peggy. It didn't matter. I accepted it graciously and later put it away.

I sat across from him in his ridiculous outfit. He was funny and wry and very charming. He had a wicked sense of humor. I knew that he was smart and considerably savvy, despite his hillbilly ways.

I'd seen photographs, one or two movies, but the reality of

meeting Elvis was still a shock to me. It had a strange, theatrical quality to it—the startling unreality of a fairy tale, as when Belle first sees the wolf-headed Beast. Elvis seemed that otherworldly to me, and in his presence my lips locked, my mind raced, my heart flew around my body, the plane flew to Tahoe, and off I went on another unknown adventure.

I'd brought along a stash of cocaine that someone had given me a few weeks before. I didn't think I could deal with him or the coming events without it. I needed my confidence—*faux* as it was. With coke, I told myself, I could forge a safe distance between us until I could figure myself out in this precarious situation. I couldn't look at Elvis for longer than a few seconds but in those brief glimpses we began to connect. By the time we got to the hotel, he had relaxed and I had softened. To my amazement, and despite all the weirdness on both sides, we seemed to actually like each other.

We started kissing right away. He must have loved to kiss because he was quite good at it. And that face pressed against mine was very handsome indeed. Surprisingly so. Little by little, I found myself becoming attracted to him. Yes, he was overweight, with a paunch, and his skin was kind of pasty, but damn he was good-looking, with his beautiful blue eyes, classic nose, and pouty mouth. We kept on kissing and then went straight into the bedroom. Elvis had the same sort of one-pointed passion that turned me on.

He was a great kisser, but that was about it. We went to bed. He smelled good and kissed like a god. Very warm, wet, and passionate. I lost myself briefly and wanted him never to stop kissing me. We were so different, but I could make him laugh.

We talked a little about his movie career. Elvis was elusive about his past but you knew without a doubt that he loved performing. He said he didn't want to do those movies anymore—"travelogues," as he called them.

"You know," I said, "you could really pursue some great roles and get them. Why don't you take acting lessons?" A glimmer of what could be lit up his face and he danced a karate dance for me. For a moment, he was happy. Just the thought of testing his own limits made him positively glow. But by the end of that first weekend I realized none of that was going to happen; his kingdom was sealed. And when I felt that door close, I wasn't sure I could stay another minute. But I did, and I went back for more.

He sat there silently for a few minutes with the TV droning on in the background. Then his dark cloud vanished as quickly as it had formed and he was his disarming self again. A heavy make-out and petting session with a teenage boy ensued—that's the way I would describe it. He didn't feel like a man next to me—more like a boy who'd never matured. The petting went on for quite a while. And then we made love. Or tried to. Elvis knew he was sexy; he just wasn't up to sex. Not that he wasn't built, but with me, at least, he was virtually impotent. Then again, who could get it up with all those drugs in him? When it came time to actually have sex and he couldn't consummate it, he became embarrassed and went into the bathroom. I knew he felt badly, because he left me a poem scrawled on a torn-off scrap of paper on my pillow.

He disappeared into the bathroom for hours. What *was* he doing in there? I sat in the bedroom in a daze. Waiting for him to emerge and forever hopeful that we could try again to make love.

At some point I looked at the torn piece of cardboard on which he had scribbled the poem. It was part of a traditional Irish blessing. "Peg," he had written:

MAY THE ROAD RISE TO MEET YOU
MAY THE WIND BE ALWAYS AT YOUR BACK
THE SUN SHINE WARM UPON YOUR FACE

For that moment Elvis had made an effort to communicate. He had been touched, he had wanted to connect. Nothing was said about the lack of sex. Conversation by now had shut down. I didn't know what Elvis was feeling. I didn't even know what he was doing for such a long time in the bathroom. Waiting in bed, I was beginning to feel trapped. I couldn't just amble out into the next room to get a breath because all his guys were in the front of the suite gearing up for show time. I could hear their piercing laughter and loud voices against the background of the blaring TV.

Elvis finally came out. He was in full ceremonial dress: pancake makeup and slicked-back, blackened hair. It was as if he had unpacked his old self and changed into someone else. Two hours earlier, I had seen him naked with his pale, nearly transparent skin. Now his belly was gone. Elvis had probably wrapped himself in some kind of girdle to bring in his waist. His blue eyes were outstandingly lined in kohl and mascara. He'd morphed. Along with his appearance, his personality changed radically. By the time he came out of the bathroom, he was King Elvis, and there was nothing to talk about.

Before I got ready to meet him at the show downstairs, I went into the bathroom and found his huge makeup kit filled with mascara, makeup, black hair dye, and pills.

When I went down to the theater where he was performing, the Memphis Mafia walked me to my seat. Elvis always had his people on you. From two to five bodyguards wherever you went. Still, it was exciting watching the show and knowing you were going home with him when every other woman there was screaming and yelling, wishing they were in your place.

Even though Elvis was past his classic period, he put on a great show. I was beginning to realize that Elvis had to be high. He must have taken drugs just to get up on stage. You could feel the energy build. That, of course, was part of his charm. He'd clown around on stage, joking with his musicians and singers, but when it came to singing, he was totally focused. It was as if the songs, the most ephemeral things that there are, were his stone reality—perhaps the only one. Given his state of mind and the drugs, I don't know how he got through a show. He would sweat profusely during the performance. A number of times during the show one of the band members would walk across the stage and tie a small silk scarf around Elvis's neck. Once it was filled with divine sweat, he would throw it off into the audience and the women would go wild. They'd scream his name and tears would pour from their eyes.

During some of his performances I stayed back in the room and slept. I had to catch up somehow. After the first couple of shows, I really didn't want to go anymore. By the second weekend in Tahoe, my desire to captivate him and alter his perspective on life was beginning to wane, too. A few nights I waited up for him. Elvis would come back from the show and go through hours and hours of winding down, and I'd sit with him and his "boys" until the morning. It was as if he had the bends and had to readjust his entire organism, joking and reviewing what funny incidents had taken place on stage. And then he'd sing, and though it wasn't my kind of music, watching him sit at the piano playing and singing his Presleyesque versions of gospel music made me smile. I had grown up on what I knew to be real rhythm and blues and I was a total, all-knowing snob in that area. But this was Elvis, after all, and who could resist his delivery?

Finally, feeling relieved, pleased with himself after a good show, and fairly relaxed, he'd eat a huge meal of bacon, fried eggs, and grits with wads of butter and pancakes with sausages—his way of coming down. Elvis ate like there was no tomorrow.

"Peg, eat something, darlin'," he'd say. "You're too skinny, baby. The wind gonna blow you away if you don't put some meat on your bones."

They'd all laugh under his encouragement. Meanwhile I was thinking, "Come on, let's play house, let's just go to bed and kiss and hug awhile and forget the world." All I wanted him to do was hold me in his arms and make love. I just wanted that closeness. We tried it again that first night after the show, but after that we gave up.

Perhaps trying to postpone the inevitable attempt at intimacy, Elvis would prolong the evening with the guys. He'd sing more songs; he'd make more jokes. Everyone would laugh as if it were the first time they'd heard them. And on and on the night went. It was a big fun game to them. There wasn't one serious thing said, but there was an undercurrent that I didn't get at first. After a couple of replays of the same situation, I began to pick up on a disturbing vibe. There was an edge of violence to these post-show sessions. As if they could have chewed up anybody and spit them out. Periodically Elvis would get aroused by the menace around him, and in between showing off his karate moves, he would take out a gun and wave it around.

Every now and again, the mischievous boy would shine through. I saw a fun-loving teenager who wanted to prank his band members with practical jokes. Whether it was a whoopie cushion placed on one of the guys' chairs or dried red peppers poured on someone's eggs, there was always a prank ready to be played.

Elvis had to have people around him at all times. He needed an audience. When he was alone he became morose and elusive. One on one, he hid. Of his entourage, Joe Esposito seemed like the most stable and grounded. Joe was his guy and the only one who seemed to have any common sense. The rest of them were just Elvis lackeys and hangers-on. Joe was also the one who called you and made the arrangements. He was someone I felt I could rely on.

Every day at about six or seven in the morning, Elvis would want a shot, and Dr. Feelgood would come to his suite with his bag of goodies. A real M.D., or at least he portrayed himself as such. Good bedside manner, an authentic black leather doctor's bag in hand. After he had his shot, Elvis came up behind me and wrapped his arms across my back.

"Peg, let the doctor give you a shot now," he said sweetly. "It'll make you feel real good." He was persuasive and of course his holding me helped fuel the possibilities of a night in bed with him. He said it would make me sleep, and I hadn't slept since I'd been there. But that night and other nights my response to his offer was always the same: no thanks. Elvis got upset. His voice was strained and his jaw tight. He became adamant that I take the shot. As if he wouldn't have anything to do with me if I didn't—or would try to force me in some way.

Eventually Elvis got so insistent about the doctor thing, I started to get paranoid. While he was off laughing with his boys I slipped into another bedroom, one with all red walls. The walls began to close in on me and I shut my eyes and prayed to get out alive and back home. I'm Dorothy, I thought, desperately wanting to get out of Oz and back to my safety net. Elvis was shouting through the door about how

I had to take one of those shots. I pretended that I'd already taken something, at which point he backed off. Maybe he'd come to his senses and realized he didn't want me to overdose in his hotel suite. I didn't want to fight with him. He had a strong, persuasive energy, and he didn't give up easily.

Had I taken the shot, I'm sure I would have either died or passed out for days. These were heavy chemical cocktails, and Elvis was seriously into them. It was beginning to dawn on me that the prerequisite for being with Elvis was to get as fucked up as he was. I wanted to run as far away as possible.

One night, Elvis finally wound down after his show and dinner and shots—and while we were in bed together he fell off into a heavy-breathing stupor. After an hour he suddenly woke up and started choking. I pulled his upper body to a sitting position. I had to drag him up with all my strength because he was like a dead weight and still passed out. Once in an upright position, he continued to choke. He coughed and spit and then started violently gagging. Oh my God, I thought, he's going to choke to death. I punched him firmly on the back and he made a final heave. I frantically turned on the light. He was white as a sheet but still breathing. In his lap, all over his silk pajamas, was vomit filled with pills and capsules. Maybe fifty or seventy-five capsules and pills of every description. Some whole, others half open—along with the contents of last night's meal. He could easily have died, not only from ingesting a near-fatal dose of pills, but also from choking on his own vomit. At the moment of crisis, he called for his mother. He sat there like a baby wailing for her. I cleaned him up and held him until he fell back to sleep. I stroked his head until I fell asleep, too, while the sun tried desperately to enter the curtained and darkened bedroom.

By the third weekend I was feeling more confused than ever. I cared for him and I knew he was in pain but I felt pissed that he wasn't doing anything about it. My feelings were being fueled by extreme dislocation, not to mention my constant chipping away at what little cocaine I had left. Sometimes I didn't know where I was. In a hotel somewhere, either Vegas or Tahoe. It was hard to tell which was which—life lived indoors with the curtains drawn. I lay there in the gloomy light, just waiting in bed for him to wake up. Elvis kept vampire's hours, a surreal existence of perpetual twilight.

On the plane with him that first weekend we flew to Lake Tahoe, there was a moment I felt impossibly hopeful and expansive about the time we might spend together. I watched him as he stared out the window. "Wouldn't it be great to just take off and go to Europe?" I asked.

"I've already been," he answered. I looked at him quizzically.

"To Germany," he said, "when I was in the Army." As if that were enough. I was dumbfounded.

Ultimately, I found I couldn't see Elvis again. He called over and over again, but I didn't take the calls. There was nothing to say. His way of life scared me. I didn't want to go that far ever again. The people around him, the drugs, the claustrophobia, the insanity before and after his performances—combined with my own obsessive use of cocaine—had all been disorienting and disturbing. A mistake. In my mind the weekends blurred together into a series of distorted and scary images. I didn't care about any of it. The only thing I cared about was his beautiful soul, but I wasn't going to be able to save him—nobody was. Besides, I had problems of my own. Who was I to save anybody?

I'M THE TEACHER

From "Elvis Presley: The Untold Story,"
an excerpt from *Elvis: We Love You Tender,*
Ladies' Home Journal, November 1979[*]

By Dee Presley, Billy Stanley,
David Stanley, and Rick Stanley

Would you trust your children with Elvis Presley? Dee (Stanley) Presley, Elvis's stepmother, did. She and her three sons tell the story of Elvis through their eyes and describe the years they spent with Elvis and what it was like to be with him on a daily, personal basis.

ATOP A HILL JUST OUTSIDE OF MEMPHIS, TENNESSEE, SITS an elegant estate of 13 rolling acres. From U.S. 51, which runs past its iron gates, the two-story, 23-room mansion, with its four graceful pillars, looks like an antebellum plantation. Elvis Presley bought Graceland for $100,000 in 1957 just as he was emerging as a star.

• • •

When Dee Stanley first saw Graceland shortly before she married Elvis's father, Vernon, she suddenly understood what marriage to Vernon Presley would mean for her three sons. The white limestone mansion, shimmering in the Tennessee light, seemed to promise the security she had lacked as an Army man's wife; it meant that her sons, Billy, Ricky and David, would be assured of college educations. *Now I can bring up my boys properly*, she thought. But Dee had no way of knowing that the notions she had about her sons' futures would never materialize.

VERNON PRESLEY WAS A 17-YEAR-OLD FARM WORKER IN MISSISSIPPI when he married Gladys Smith. On January 8, 1935, she gave birth to identical twin boys. The firstborn was named Elvis Aron Presley. The second, Jessie, was stillborn. From the moment of Elvis's birth until his mother's death 23 years later, the relationship between mother and son was unusually devoted. Elvis would eventually develop a close bond with his father's second wife, Dee Stanley.

Dee, a vivacious, petite blonde, first met Vernon in Germany; she was with her husband, Bill Stanley, an Army officer. Vernon was with Elvis, who was stationed on Stanley's base during his hitch in the Army. There was an immediate affinity between Dee and Vernon, which led to her divorce from Stanley and subsequent marriage to Elvis's father. In 1960, Dee moved into Graceland with her three young sons, Billy, Ricky and David.

If the three boys had a stepfather in Vernon Presley, they would have a surrogate father and male model in Elvis. But sadly, the effect he was to have on their lives was unforeseeable.

Elvis first met his stepbrothers when he returned to Graceland from the Army, in 1960. Billy was eight, Ricky, seven and David, five.

"I like you boys," he said gently. "I like you very much." He picked them up, one by one, and hugged them.

Elvis had always wanted brothers—his twin brother's stillbirth left him with a feeling that he had lost a part of himself. It was this feeling, perhaps, that caused him to give the Stanley boys such a warm welcome.

DEE OBJECTS

RICK WAS ONLY 16 YEARS OLD WHEN ELVIS ASKED HIM TO BE HIS personal aide and valet. Dee objected strongly. She wanted her sons to stay in school—and of the three boys, Rick had the most academic promise.

"Ricky is going to be a doctor, Elvis," she said, stiffening. "I want him to study medicine. He can't just be wasted; he's a very intellectual young man."

"If you'll just let him come with me, " Elvis pleaded, "he'll have a teacher, he'll have Bible classes, and I'll have a limousine ready to take him to church every Sunday. I'll send him to college." Elvis looked at Dee sweetly, and smiled. "I'll always take care of your boys, Dee. You *know* that."

Rick Stanley was 16 when he stepped onto the plane with Elvis Presley. The youngest person in the entourage next to Rick was 28. "I was pretty impressed when I heard about the teacher and everything," he says. "Mom wasn't going for it, but there wasn't much she could say."

When they were on the plane, sitting next to each other, Elvis turned to Rick and laughed. *"I'm* the teacher," he said.

For Dee Presley, this was the beginning of what she calls, "living in a fool's paradise." Everything her son did on the road with Elvis was carefully concealed from her.

"I could never get Ricky back after that," she says. "Then Billy went, and then David, too. Elvis bought them cars; he bought them motorcycles, horses and other expensive gifts that took them further and further away from me. I wasn't ready for my sons to be introduced to that kind of life. Every moral and belief that I taught them was taken away."

For Rick and his brothers, it was the beginning of a unique education—life on the road with Elvis was a blur of hard work, high jinks, alcohol, drugs and women, with rock 'n' roll music providing the background. "It was like a constant high on cocaine," Rick says.

It was also a once-in-a-lifetime opportunity to see the world through the eyes of the man who had become an idol to his generation. The highs with "The Boss" would be the highest imaginable; the lows, the most abysmal. Tragically, the brothers would eventually witness firsthand Elvis Presley's destruction.

"TCB" was what life around Elvis Presley was about. It meant simply "Taking Care of Business"—Elvis's business. Anything that ever needed to be done—from routing, organization and logistics of a multimillion-dollar road show to making sure that The Boss had tissues in his bathroom—came under the TCB heading. As Rick puts it, "TCB-ing meant being on constant alert to Elvis's every need. We got to know exactly when he wanted a glass of water or a cigar, without him having to ask for it." At concerts, the responsibility of protecting Elvis was enormous. He loved his fans, but their enthusiasm sometimes bordered on dementia.

"Girls would come at you like wildcats, and it was my job to stop them," says Billy, who worked stage security for a time. "You would see fifteen or twenty coming at you at once. Some of the ladies would conk us over the head with umbrellas or purses."

One night during a performance in Las Vegas, five men suddenly rose from the audience to mount the stage. Elvis lashed out with a karate kick that disabled one of the attackers. The stage was suddenly aswarm with bodyguards and police. All five men were arrested, and others in the audience were held for questioning.

It was the beginning of a constant stream of threats—bombings, assassinations, kidnappings.

While Presley's entourage closed ranks around him, he took his own precautions. On any given night, if you had frisked Elvis on stage, you would have found a four-shot derringer in his boot or behind his belt buckle. If he went for an automobile ride, he might carry a .357 Magnum in a shoulder holster, and a .45 automatic tucked in his belt.

One day, Presley told David that he was going to be his personal bodyguard. "We're groomin' you, David. You're gonna be the best bodyguard I ever had."

By the age of 20, David was packing a .357 Magnum and had earned a black belt in karate. He became The Boss's "headhunter"—the man who always walked in front of Elvis in crowds.

"He wouldn't go anywhere without me," says David, whom Presley dubbed "Charles Manson." "He knew how I felt about him. There was an emotional bond between us, and Elvis knew I would never hesitate to put my life before his." That, apparently, was part of the arrangement. Elvis even asked David how he felt about it.

"David, would you die for me?" he asked.

"Yes, sir," was the reply.

NEVER COMPROMISED

PRESLEY NEVER COMPROMISED ON HIS ROAD TO THE TOP. HE KNEW no moderation in anything he did. In school, he was an outsider. Ignoring all codes of behavior of the time, he dressed in loud clothes and wore his hair long. To the tough, crew cut, redneck kids at school, Elvis looked like something from outer space or the homosexual community. Having been prey to vicious ridicule, he never forgot the humiliation of his youth. When he graduated from high school, in 1953, he had a burning ambition to step beyond the limitations of his poor beginnings. By 1954, at age 19, he had cut "All Right Mama," and things were never the same after that.

Presley recorded hit after hit and rapidly became a millionaire. He stocked his life with clothes, cars and new friends, meanwhile developing the codes of manhood that would stay with him for the rest of his life.

Violence was part of his conception of true manhood. David remembers driving with Elvis past a service station in Los Angeles where several men were loitering. One of them insulted the singer. He braked to a screeching stop, jumped out and, approaching the ringleader, said, "I don't like people talking to me like that." When the man cursed back, Presley knocked him to the ground with a vicious karate attack. The other men stood quietly as Presley got in his car and drove away.

Elvis resorted to extreme measures when anyone or anything got in his way, but with women, he was always respectful and attentive—never pushy. His sincere, country boy manner worked every time. "He liked a wholesome, refined type of woman," says Rick. "A neat appearance was important, no smoking, no bad language, no drinking. . . . If he saw a woman with a beer can in her hand he would cringe."

A teen-ager he had met when he was with the Army in Germany fitted the bill perfectly and he couldn't forget her. Priscilla Beaulieu, daughter of an Air Force officer, was not quite 15 years old at the time and beautiful. Her hair was a mane of brown curls, and she had a little button nose.

It took Presley six years to get around to proposing to "Cilla"— they married on May 1, 1967. Exactly nine months later, they gave birth to a six-pound, 15-ounce girl. Dee remembers visiting the maternity ward in Memphis's Baptist Memorial Hospital with Vernon and Elvis.

"She looked at us with those blue eyes," says Dee, "and Elvis's face lit up like a beacon."

Elvis was proud of his wife and daughter—so much so that he kept them virtually locked up at Graceland while he set his own standard of behavior on the road.

Presley was becoming more and more convinced that his money could buy him everything he wanted—including women, friends, immunities.

On one occasion, Elvis decided he wanted Rick's girlfriend of many years, Jill. Approaching Rick, Elvis said: "Look, I want to go out with Jill. Do you mind?"

"Not her, Elvis! *Not her!*"

"Tell you what," Presley said. "How would you like a new car— anything?" Elvis backed off when Rick threatened to find another job.

Presley spent his money to make other people happy, because he was bored, to shock people or because someone (usually his father) told him not to.

"He always went all out," Rick says. He didn't buy one car, he bought a fleet. He didn't buy one airplane, he bought the biggest and a lot of them.

"He was rich enough to do almost anything. If something displeased him on TV, or if he wanted to startle someone, he would pick up a handgun and blow the set away."

WIDE RELIGIOUS INTERESTS

IN HIS YOUTH, ELVIS PRESLEY HAD BEEN INTERESTED IN FUNDAMENtalist Christianity, convinced that he could go far if he had faith in God. He wore a crucifix and a Star of David on the same gold chain—and when asked why, replied: "I don't want to miss out on heaven because of a technicality."

He delved into the ancient philosophies of the Far East, particularly Buddhism, meditation and yoga, as well as the more modern teachings of Scientology and other offshoots of the human potential movement.

Presley enjoyed reading about the great mystics, spiritualists and psychics and was fascinated by psychokinesis, mind control, numerology and astrology. His mini-library on metaphysics, contained in two portable bookcases, went with him everywhere. He believed in reincarnation.

Soon, Presley gained a reputation for having "powers"— psychic, spiritual, other-worldly. The singer himself believed that he had faith healing powers.

Finally, Elvis Presley had a deeply ingrained fascination with death. He wanted to "understand" it and turned to a study of death.

His curiosity led him into mortuaries, where he learned about embalming. He pored through volume after volume on the subject. "He called death the best thing that could happen to you," says Billy. "He often said how glad he'd be to see his mom when he got to heaven," adds Rick.

IF THE MEN AROUND ELVIS WERE TO TAKE CARE OF BUSINESS, THE women were expected to provide Tender Loving Care, particularly when the men returned from a tour.

"Elvis loved the idea of having a woman back home waiting for him," Billy says. But that desire extended beyond his own wife, Priscilla. Ann Hill, Billy's 18-year-old wife, was often at Graceland. She had auburn hair, blue eyes and alabaster skin, and she was the first love of Billy's life. But there was a chemistry between Ann and Elvis, evident to everyone except Billy.

"Elvis would often call and ask Annie to come over to join him at the pool," Billy remembers. "Then he would call and send me on some errand."

The affair, when it happened, shocked Billy's family. Dee couldn't bring herself to tell her son that Ann was being unfaithful, and worse, that the man was Elvis, whom Billy loved and trusted.

After a month, Elvis tired of Annie and banished her from his house. She vented her anger on Billy, who couldn't understand why she was so bad-tempered. Her complaints became more and more cutting until one day it slipped out:

"How would you feel if I told you that I had been involved with Elvis?" Annie asked defiantly. Billy was shaken.

Shortly after, Elvis decided Billy's presence in the TCB group disturbed him and told Vernon to lay him off. The resulting estrangement lasted for the rest of Elvis's life.

"I felt like such a fool," Billy says now. "I couldn't believe Elvis would do something like that."

"Elvis was just not a fair husband," maintains Rick. "He would go out and cheat on his wife while she was 'locked' up at Graceland. It was rough for her, especially since Elvis was a jealous man—he knew how men could be, and didn't trust them when it came to Priscilla . . ."

Priscilla was aware of the double standard in her marriage. She knew Elvis had other women, but in Rick's opinion it was not the "other women" that ultimately destroyed their marriage.

"I talked to Priscilla after it was all over, and she said, 'Ricky, I'm a woman. I need somebody there.' She needed love and affection. She also needed a home where she could be with Elvis without a bunch of guys always hanging around."

The clubhouse atmosphere that often prevailed at Graceland made intimacy between Elvis and his wife impossible. Priscilla didn't like some of the men who worked for her husband. She left Presley in February, 1972.

A year later, Elvis filed for divorce. The decree was granted in October, 1973. Priscilla was granted custody of Lisa Marie Presley, then five years old.

After the divorce—seen by some as the turning point in Elvis's life—his career started downhill.

In Presley's final years, drugs played a destructive role. "The man was into drugs, and so was I," Rick says. "I'm not ashamed to talk about it, because I've changed. Elvis had a lot of problems. I loved the man. Now I think it's important for the public to know the truth."

It was while Elvis was serving his overseas hitch with the Army that he discovered amphetamines. Benzedrine and Dexedrine were dispensed by the millions during World War II to soldiers facing combat, to keep them alert and moving forward. The drugs were still being used, covertly if not officially, when Elvis was stationed in Germany in 1959. A sergeant would hand them out before maneuvers.

"Elvis told me that he brought home two trunks full of Dexedrine," Rick says.

"Speed," or "uppers" as amphetamines are known on the street, give the user a sense of being "up," and not needing food for long periods. Elvis became a habitual user during the 1960s. He felt drugs helped him meet the demands of his grueling schedule and soon mounted the destructive seesaw: "Uppers" to get going, narcotics to unwind, "uppers" again to banish morning grogginess.

"Sleeping medication" became the TCB euphemism for the various narcotics Elvis began taking, which included Quaaludes and class-A narcotics like Demerol and Dilaudid.

The drugs in Elvis's life moved quickly from use to abuse in the early 1970s. "There was no real kick for Elvis to get into," Rick says, "so he got into drugs."

Elvis's narcotics and amphetamines were all legally prescribed for him by a slew of doctors, and this seemed to provide him with a sanction, a further rationale that they were justified. Rick explains: "He had about four or five doctors who gave him anything he wanted. All they appeared to care about were the cars and other gifts he gave them for writing the prescriptions."

In Elvis's mind, his drugs were legal and necessary; Rick's weren't. When Presley saw his brother delving further into hard drugs, he stipulated: "Cut it out or get out!" Elvis regarded smoking marijuana as a moral weakness. "Don't do it on tours," he would say to his reefer-smoking brother. "It's against the law." Rick, well aware of the contents of Presley's medicine cabinet, saw the hypocrisy in his brother's warnings.

In 1975, the conflict came to a head, and Rick walked out the gate. But eight months later, when he was arrested for presenting a forged prescription, Elvis was the first to come to his aid; the two were then reconciled.

Rick understood Elvis's step from capsule to hypodermic needle better than anyone else around Presley. By the time Elvis's habit became serious, Rick had already kicked his. He became frightened when he saw how Presley was using drugs, knowing where it would head. "I've never seen anybody who could take it like that," he says. "You just don't do dope like he did and live through it."

The power and nature of Elvis's drugs were what worried Rick. "In 1972–73, he started getting into needles. His body looked like a pincushion. He never stuck anything into his veins because they were too shallow—he'd go into the muscle, and it wasn't only drugs. Sometimes he'd shoot vitamin B-12, but mostly it was the same drugs I did—Tuinal, Demerol and Dilaudid. He was addicted, for sure. He enjoyed the high."

The others around Elvis were as powerless as Rick in influencing Elvis's behavior. Aides and his personal physician, Dr. George Nichopoulos, would frequently raid his medicine cabinet to substitute harmless mixtures of vitamins for barbiturates, but that proved ineffective because Presley usually knew or had too many outside sources who could speedily replace them.

OUTGROWTH OF TCB

RICK WAS IN A PRECARIOUS POSITION—PRESLEY KNEW HE WAS A former addict and, as he didn't like to inject himself with the drugs, he had Rick do it for him. The administering of drugs became an outgrowth of TCB.

"Sure," Rick sighs, "I did it for him all the time. David did, too. A lot of people will say, 'Well, if you *loved* the man, how could you have done it? Why didn't you try to tell him?' After a while, he just didn't want to hear it. You could not get through to him. There were times when I protested, but in the long run I was devoted to the man—to doing his bidding—and I would do whatever he wanted me to do. Many times I had to help pull him through and keep him alive when we thought he wasn't going to make it. He'd fall asleep sometimes while eating and nearly choke to death on his food."

Another problem was Elvis would occasionally wake up, forget that he had taken his medication and then take more. "Sometimes I'd find him on his back on the floor," says David. "I'd carry him to his room. We'd pull the covers over him and stay with him."

Elvis took his "sleeping medication" just before bedtime. One of the men in his entourage would be on night duty to watch over him, unless there was a woman there; then she was responsible.

For almost five years after his divorce the woman often would be Linda Thompson. She was girlfriend, trusted companion and, if necessary, nurse.

"She couldn't have come at a better time in Elvis's life," Rick says fondly. "He was hurtin' from the divorce, and needed someone."

It was Joe Esposito, an aide, Rick and Dr. Nichopoulos who convinced Elvis to be hospitalized and dry out. There were two weeks in October, 1973, two weeks in January and February, 1975, and two more weeks in August and September of that year when he was admitted to the hospital in Memphis. Reasons of health were released to the public—fatigue, enlarged colon, stomach inflammation, gastroenteritis . . . "Every time he went in it was to dry out from drugs," says Rick. "You can cover it up as much as you want. They would slowly try to cut him off his medications. I thought it was ridiculous because they'd cut him off but still give him small amounts. If they wanted to dry him out, I didn't understand why they couldn't cut him off completely just like they did with me. It's rough, but it's the only way you can do it.

"We had to filter out some of his employees when he was hospitalized," recalls Rick, "because they would take drugs into him. They'd get gifts for it, you know, cars . . ."

Even with all the doctors and employees involved, it was ultimately up to Elvis to stop using drugs.

Elvis Presley would spend the last and most tragic year of his life with Ginger Alden—a woman with whom he had little in common, and even less to talk about. Presley insiders felt that, unlike Linda, she didn't understand what was happening to Elvis. When the end came she would be in bed asleep.

NOCTURNAL LIFE

ELVIS NOW LIVED A NOCTURNAL LIFE, NEVER SEEING SUNSHINE AND shunning exercise. As performance time approached for his Las Vegas shows, he rode an elevator down 30 floors from his suite to a golf cart, which carried him through back corridors to the stage.

"He was bedridden during the daytime the last year," Rick

recalls sadly. "We'd fly to a city and he'd get into bed as soon as we got there. We'd get him up to do the show. Back on the plane, he'd get right into bed again."

Audiences were noticing Elvis's puffy appearance. Critics savaged him. But even at the very end, on his last few tours, Elvis was still able to draw enough energy to dazzle his public.

In the summer of 1977, the singer returned to Memphis from what would be his last tour to spend a few weeks at Graceland before flying off to do a show in Oregon. Ginger Alden was spending her nights with him. David and Rick were on duty, alternating nights and days on call for Presley.

Sometime before 6 A.M. on August 16, Elvis handed Rick a prescription for Dilaudid capsules and sent him to a drugstore to get it filled. Then he and Rick spent some time alone together. Presley was in the mood for prayer. Around six o'clock they sat on the singer's bed, clasped their hands together as they had often done before and closed their eyes.

Elvis prayed aloud. "Lord help me to have insight, and forgive me my sins. Dear God, please help me to get back when I feel down like this, and to always strive for good in the world. In the name of Jesus Christ. Amen."

Rick nodded his Amen.

"Ricky," Elvis said, "tell David when he comes on duty not to disturb me under any circumstances. I don't want to get up until four P.M. I need plenty of rest for the tour."

At 2:30 P.M. that day, when Ginger woke, she found Elvis collapsed on the bathroom floor from an apparent heart attack. Paramedics rushed him to Baptist Memorial Hospital for shock treatments—the last hope.

At 3:30 on the afternoon of August 16, 1977, Elvis Aron Presley was pronounced dead—he was 42 years old. It was all over.

The body was taken to the hospital morgue for autopsy. During the preliminary stage of the examination, Dr. Jerry Francisco, Shelby County Coroner, said that cardiac arrhythmia and coronary disease were the natural causes of death. He also said, according to *The New York Times*, that Elvis had a history of mild hypertension. "But the specific cause may not be known for a week or two, pending lab studies. It is possible in cases like this that the specific cause may never be known."

PRESCRIBED DRUGS ONLY

AT A PRESS CONFERENCE, REPORTERS ASKED DR. FRANCISCO WHETHER the autopsy had indicated drug abuse. According to *The New York Times* of August 17, 1977, Dr. Francisco said that: "The only drugs he had detected were those that had been prescribed by Mr. Presley's personal physician for hypertension and a blockage of the colon, for which he had been hospitalized twice in 1975."

There was no mention made of the Dilaudid that Elvis had taken that morning. And Rick's version of Presley's hospitalization in 1975 was that both incidents were to "cut off" his sleeping medication.

Several medical scenarios for the death were plausible, all of which, if they were investigated and pursued, were never made public because the ruling of "natural causes" at the preliminary autopsy quashed forever the possibility of a public inquest into the death and assured that all future findings would remain within the Presley family.

One thing is certain: There were enough things allegedly wrong with Elvis at the time of the autopsy to make it extremely difficult for the examiners to determine the exact cause of death. Moreover, regardless of what drugs may have been detected, there was also enough coronary damage so that it was just as likely that Elvis had succumbed to heart difficulty as anything else. David thinks there might have been a "strong possibility" that Elvis overdosed on his medication when he got up that morning. It had, after all, been known to occur, and he recalls several times when he found Elvis unconscious on his bathroom floor in similar instances.

It would, of course, be irresponsible to point a finger at anyone in the absence of concrete information but much would seem to contradict the initial public statements of certain officials. It is unlikely, however, that such contradictions will ever be cleared up.

I GOT A CALL
FROM ELVIS PRESLEY

From "The White House-Graceland
Connection That Might Have Saved Elvis,"
The New Yorker, August 18, 1997[*]

By Douglas Brinkley

Another strange encounter between a U.S.
president and Elvis from acclaimed historian
Douglas Brinkley.

T HOUSANDS OF DEVOTED FANS AROUND THE COUNTRY WILL gather this week to mark the twentieth anniversary of Elvis Presley's death, but it is unlikely that any of them will feel that perhaps they might just have been able to save the king of rock and roll. That distinction—sort of—belongs to President Jimmy Carter.

"When I was first elected President, I got a call from Elvis Presley," Carter told me recently. "He was totally stoned and didn't know what he was saying. His sentences were almost incoherent." It was the summer of 1977, and Elvis, in a rage fuelled by barbiturates, had telephoned the White House from Graceland (among the two

• • •

*Reprinted by permission of International Creative Management, Inc., copyright © 1997 by Douglas Brinkley most visited residences in America) seeking a Presidential pardon for a sheriff he knew who was in some legal trouble. "I talked to him for a long time, and I finally extracted that from him," Carter recalled. In a scene wildly reminiscent of the "Saturday Night Live" sketch in which the thirty-ninth President (played by Dan Aykroyd) used the White House hot line to talk a teen-ager down from a bad acid trip, Carter said he patiently tried to ease Presley out of his paranoid delusions, calming his fears that he was being "shadowed" by sinister forces and that his friend was being framed.

Carter was no stranger to rock stars. Throughout the 1976 Presidential campaign, his friendships with the Allman Brothers and Bob Dylan helped loosen up his image, and he once told an audience that his understanding of "what's right and wrong in this society" came from listening to such Dylan numbers as "The Times, They Are a-Changin'." The former Georgia governor was also an unabashed admirer of Elvis Presley's music. Jimmy and Rosalynn Carter went to see Elvis perform at the Atlanta Omni in 1973. They went backstage afterward, and Carter embraced the King, despite his sheen of sweat and makeup. "And then I declared Elvis Presley Day in Georgia," Carter said. "I noticed in Graceland they have got that declaration signed by me on the wall."

Given this history—and considering Presley's familiarity with Richard Nixon, who had made him an honorary U.S. Drug Enforcement Agent in 1970—it wasn't so far-fetched for the King to telephone the Oval Office with a personal problem. Carter recalled, "I asked him what the sheriff's sentence was, and he said that he hadn't been tried in court yet. Well I said, 'Elvis, I can't consider a pardon until after a trial and sentencing and everything.' I don't think he understood that." (It was never clear that Elvis's friend was in trouble anyway.) But he didn't stop: though Presley's desperate calls to the White House continued unabated, Carter never spoke to him again.

A few weeks later, on August 16th, Elvis Presley died, at the age of forty-two. There was a debate within the White House over whether a Presidential condolence statement was appropriate, given that the star was a known drug abuser. Elvis's importance was beyond doubt: his death was such a big story that both ABC and NBC led their newscasts with it. CBS opted to go with Gerald Ford's support of the Panama Canal treaties. The executive producer of CBS News, Burton Benjamin, Jr., later lamented that his tombstone would read, "This is the man who did not lead with Elvis Presley."

Carter himself was never in doubt, and the White House released the following statement: "Elvis Presley's death deprives our country of a part of itself. He was . . . a symbol to people the world over of the vitality, rebelliousness, and good humor of his country." As Elvis's funeral procession wound its way through the streets of Memphis, Jimmy Carter, at home in the White House, mourned along with countless other fans. "It was a sad day for the Republic," the former President now says about the pop icon he wonders if he could have saved.

VERY DEVOTED
TO ELVIS

From *I Called Him Babe: Elvis Presley's
Nurse Remembers*, Chapter 11[*]

By Marian J. Cocke

Marian J. Cocke was one of Elvis's nurses at Graceland, in charge of administering his medication, which was prescribed to him by Elvis's personal physician, Dr. George C. Nichopoulos (aka Dr. Nick). Dr. Nick was put on trial in 1980, charged with fourteen counts of overprescribing drugs to Elvis, Jerry Lee Lewis, and others. During the trial, it was revealed that in 1977 alone, Dr. Nick had written 199 prescriptions totaling more than 10,000 doses of sedatives, amphetamines, and narcotics in Elvis's name. He was acquitted on all counts as the jury concluded he had tried to act in Elvis's best interests.

• • •

MEDICATIONS

ELVIS WAS ON A NUMBER OF MEDICATIONS. I DO NOT REMEMBER the exact medication that he received, but he was getting medication for hypertension, his colon problem, and (as well as I remember) a medication to keep his heart rate down to normal. All of these medications were what a doctor would give to any patient who had the same health problems Elvis had.

When he was first admitted to the hospital under my care, he was having discomfort and did receive a narcotic—by injection—for this pain. He was monitored, as are all patients receiving this medication, and his was ordered "every four hours PRN." PRN means "when necessary." Thus it is very important that "PRN" be inscribed after the "four hours"; otherwise it means that a patient is to receive the medication every four hours, not just when necessary. His definitely was PRN.

There were several times when he would have the medication every four hours, as the doctor's order was written, but there were just as many times when he would not have the injection for a long period of time because he was not feeling enough pain to take it. Even before he left the hospital, this narcotic was pretty much a thing of the past, and he was receiving only the standard medications ordered for his colon problem, not any narcotic.

Shortly after I began going to Graceland, there was a flare-up of his colon problem and his cramping pain returned. Dr. Nick brought us some codeine tablets, which Kathy and I carefully monitored, keeping a list of when we gave them and counting them twice daily. We never came up short in our count. The codeine did not agree with Elvis, and we had to ask Dr. Nick for another type of medication.

This was also charted and accounted for daily by us, and it was necessary to administer it only for two or three days.

Elvis required medication in order to get to sleep more than for anything else. Remember that he was a big man, and often we gave him two sleeping capsules where an average (smaller) man might have required only one. There were times when he would come in several hours later, wide awake, and ask for another sleeping pill. This kind of thing can happen anytime, anyplace, with any patient. When he would be out all night playing racquet ball and going to a movie and was not home before I left to go to the hospital, I would put out a "doggie bag" for him. This bag held the medication for his blood pressure and his colon problem, which he was to take that morning, as well as sleeping medication he could take if he needed it. Usually he did take it, but sometimes it would still be on his bedside table when I got there in the evening.

Elvis ate a lot of salt on his food. Salt causes the retention of fluids in the body, and the amount he ate contributed greatly to making him puffy. We had a medication to make him eliminate some of this fluid—the same medication that thousands of people take every day—but it made him feel weak. One day when we were talking about his puffiness, he told me that the medication sapped his strength so much that he felt bad after taking it. He found the puffiness easier to tolerate than the weakness. We got a salt substitute for him, and he used it a lot. Often, however, he would still use the regular salt because he said it tasted better.

At no time during the months I spent at Graceland did I ever see any narcotic or barbiturate that was not prescribed by Dr. Nick for some specific problem, and these Dr. Nick gave strict orders about administering. However, if there were other medications ordered by another physician we were not aware of them, and such a thing happening would be very difficult for me to believe as there was never a time I saw Elvis when he appeared to be under the influence of drugs. Dr. Nick was very devoted to Elvis and extremely concerned about his welfare. He was very protective of him and cared for him as he would a younger brother. We followed Dr. Nick's specific instructions, and there was never a time that I noted any sort of medication abuse or misuse. As I previously stated, Kathy Seamon and I carefully monitored all his medications, regardless of what they were. There were no needle marks on his body other than the few we put there, and the skin on his arms and legs was unbroken.

Let me tell another thing about Elvis. He was difficult to stick for any type of lab work, as he was very muscular and his veins were deeply embedded and small. I learned this when he was first admitted to my care in January of 1975. He had been in the hospital before I met him, and he knew Estelle Claiborne, who was in charge of the lab pick-up team. When a blood sample was needed, we called her. Elvis said that she was the only person who had ever been able to stick him, and he was right. She was certainly the expert and was able to obtain blood samples when no one else could.

I saw this demonstrated on one occasion. One day one of the residents told Elvis that he could stick him, and he had brought the necessary items. I stood watching. The resident probed and Elvis never batted an eye, but I squirmed and gripped my hands behind my back until I couldn't stand to watch any more. Finally I walked out, called Estelle, and she came immediately and drew the necessary blood on the first try. Elvis said later, "If you have to have any more lab work, you be sure to get Mrs. Claiborne because nobody else is going to stick me!"

Another thing I have often heard concerning his health is that he ate nothing but junk food. This was not true. When he was in the hospital, Carol Kidney, the dietician, came to visit Elvis daily. She would come up every morning, talk to him about his meals, and get his requests for the day. She made various suggestions about some of his requests, and he was very cooperative in every way. He usually ate pretty much the same thing and didn't want a lot of variety, but nevertheless, he ate well. He would usually have strawberries, bacon, eggs, toast (which he ate sparingly), and coffee for breakfast. Lunch and dinner were about the same usually; he wanted hamburger steaks, creamed potatoes, string beans or spinach, and a salad. Sometimes he asked for a bacon-burger and hash browns at night, but that certainly was not "junk food."

Carol always tried to vary his tray, when possible, and she spent a lot of time seeing that he got not only what he liked, but also what he needed. We have a great dietary department, and they certainly went all out for Elvis as they do for all patients.

At Graceland I never noticed him eating junk food. He was careful about his diet and usually ate balanced meals.

The coroner's report stated that Elvis died of a heart attack and that he had an enlarged heart. This was no surprise to me. Elvis had the biggest heart of anyone I've ever known. He was both generous and compassionate, and his love for people was tremendous. Thus this seems the appropriate way for him to have gone. In my opinion, he had one other fatal illness—loneliness.

ETERNAL LIFE

From "Elvis Forever!," *TV Guide,*
August 17–23, 2002*

By William F. Buckley Jr.

The conservative author and commentator
tours Graceland on the twenty-fifth anniversary
of Elvis's death.

W HEN I VISITED GRACELAND, I WAS SHOWN ALL THE
conventional rooms, outbuildings, promenades,
collections, play courts, exhibits. I then came upon
the cordon that stretches across the staircase leading up to the living
quarters. I said to my host, Jack Soden, who runs the entire enter-
prise, could he take me upstairs? No, he said. It is a flat rule, nobody
is allowed up there. "I even turned down Vice President Gore when
he asked me." I understood, and Jack Soden understood, in turn, my
curiosity to see where Elvis had actually last been alive.

It was just after two in the afternoon of August 16, 1977—early
in the day, by Elvis's standards. His girlfriend, finding him gone from
the bedroom, thought to look for him in his vast bathroom, knocked,
got no answer and opened the door. He was lying on the floor. She

• • •

called out for help. Efforts to bring him to life were adamantly futile—they kept on trying even in the ambulance, even though they knew that the King was dead. A half hour later, at Baptist Memorial Hospital, the people began to assemble. The physicians first, then the special friends and family. Then the press, then the fans. One problem was to communicate the fact of his death officially to the assembly. The two people assigned the job couldn't get on with it; they broke down. Finally it was done by a medical technician.

Those last hours—the last weeks and months, really—were nothing to spend time on, let alone to celebrate. When a legendary hero dies after a winner-take-all struggle with a disease that wracks him in mind and body, you don't really want to go upstairs and look down on the scene where he had drawn his last breath. Elvis's body was a battleground of drugs and a wasteland of self-indulgence. Better to think of him—why not?—as a man who died from eating one too many chocolate bars. That's the best way to think of what did him in.

A couple of hours after midnight, he had summoned two or three members of his entourage (never mind that they had been asleep) because he thought he'd play a little racquetball. Elvis wanted the company he wanted when he wanted it. They played for a while, then he horsed around a bit with Billy, his cousin. He aimed his racket wrong and hit himself on the shin: "Boy, that hurts." Billy countered playfully, "If it ain't bleedin', it ain't hurting," quoting one of Elvis's favorite lines. Elvis laughed and threw his racket at him.

Then, around dawn, he sat down at the piano in the lounge area. He played a few notes, a tune or two, and then went with Willie Nelson's mournful "Blue Eyes Crying in the Rain." He loved those sad songs, and he had a lot to be sad about. That included the terrible reviews he had been getting on his tours. They were saying that he had lost his genius, that he was fat and bored, that his memory was slipping. He handled that problem, and most others, by getting more pills from Dr. Nick, aka Dr. George Nichopoulos, his personal physician. The doctors at the morgue fancied up a death certificate that nicely obscured what had gone on in his system. The BioScience lab people even disguised the name of the patient whose stomach they had plumbed; but after a while it leaked that "Ethel Moore" was really Elvis Presley, and that 14 drugs had been found in his system. When Elvis died, the mourning was deep.

And yet Elvis Presley has eternal life. It's everything about Elvis, not just his songs, that some people want, many of them not even alive when he died. Six hundred thousand people visit Graceland every year, and half of them are under 35. Elvis Presley Enterprises has 110 licenses out, marketing over 700 products. Carol Butler, who is the director of licensing, has an efficient way of putting it: "He is the world's best-selling artist, having sold more than one billion albums and singles worldwide." On June 21, Walt Disney Pictures released "Lilo & Stitch," an animated adventure featuring five of the King's recordings.

Check out the Web site, we're told: Elvis.com. You can buy an Elvis bed that "evokes the golden age of Hollywood." Other signature pieces are "a platinum-record mirror and a leather platform bed." Jalapeño Chicks is on the market with a BBQ spice, Jailhouse Rock; a Cajun spice, King Creole; and an all-purpose seasoning called G.I. Blues. Clothes of every sort bear his imprint. If you want one of *everything* Elvis-minded, don't forget the Zippo lighter with a silk-screen design. It's $130. Elvis wouldn't have used one because he didn't smoke. He didn't approve of smoking. He hardly ever drank. You see, he opposed drugs. He talked President Nixon into giving him a badge in the Drug Enforcement Agency. When he called on Nixon in the White House, Elvis wore his new jeweled, oversize glasses. He had on a dark Edwardian jacket with brass buttons. It draped like a cape around his shoulders, above a purple velvet V neck with matching pants. These were set off by the massive gold belt presented to him by a grateful hotel in Las Vegas. Over a collared, open-neck white shirt, he wore the gold lion's head pendant he had recently purchased in Beverly Hills. Why did he dress up the way he did, including the $25,000 glittery jumpsuits on display at Graceland? Because, as he had told Sam Phillips, who began it all in his little recording studio in 1953, he liked to be himself.

He certainly succeeded. The Uninhibited Man. He began as a shy, even timid postulant, an 18-year-old who just wanted to sing and kept looking for a break. Marion Keisker worked for the Phillips recording studio and had a radio talk show on the side. One day she asked the kid who kept coming in to try out one more song on a $3.98 acetate. "What kind of a singer are you?" "I sing all kinds." She persisted: "Who do you sound like?"

"I don't sound like nobody."

That was conceded by the critics just one year later.

This year, as an anniversary present, a fresh Elvis record, a remix of "A Little Less Conversation," reached No. 1 in the U.K. What made that special for the world of Elvis is that the King outdistanced the Beatles. He has more No. 1 singles than any artist in the history of the U.K.—to say it again, more even than the beloved Beatles (18 versus 17). RCA/BMG will just keep going with it. Next is a new album: *Elvis 30 #1 Hits.*

Yes, he was the King of Rock and Roll. But many who care deeply about his music *most* admire Elvis the balladeer—the Elvis of "One Night With You," to pick out only one of the songs that sing out love and loneliness, and inspire love and dispel loneliness.

HE DOESN'T LOOK ANYTHING LIKE HIMSELF

From "Graceland," *Rolling Stone,*
September 22, 1977[*]

By Caroline Kennedy

Caroline Kennedy, the then twenty-year-old daughter of John F. and Jackie Kennedy, was either part of the crowd outside Graceland the day after Elvis died and was invited inside or she called Graceland and asked if she could come pay her respects. Either way, the Presley family had no idea she would then write this article.

CLOSE FRIENDS AND RELATIVES BID THEIR PRIVATE FARE-wells to Elvis Presley at the 18-room-mansion he called Graceland.

Police and private guards sealed off the estate, which had been visited by an estimated 75,000 fans on August 17th, the day before

• • •

the funeral. Out front, a steady stream of traffic moved along Elvis Presley Boulevard, while those closest to him moved through the mansion.

Earlier that afternoon I'd been talking with some other people who were waiting to pay their respects and their mood had been quiet and restrained. Now, as they wandered around in the dark, they seemed looser, no longer afraid of losing their place in line.

Winslow "Buddy" Chapman, the director of police who looked like the advance man from *Nashville*, invited me into the house where a scarlet carpeted hall led into a large room filled with gold and white folding chairs. At the far end of the room was the gleaming copper coffin that contained the body of Elvis Presley. His face seemed swollen and his sideburns reached his chin.

"He doesn't look anything like himself," the woman beside me said softly. "He just doesn't look anything like himself. . . ."

A couple in their late 20s stood beside the casket. The woman was sobbing. The man had his arm around her. Behind the coffin, an arch led to another room where a clear-glass statue of a nude woman stood high off the floor, twirling slowly, adorned by glass beads that looked like water. Potted plastic palms surrounded the coffin and on the wall was a painting of a skyline on black velveteen.

The plantation-style mansion was large and ornate. The entrance to the dining room was framed by floor-to-ceiling scarlet drapes tied with gold tassels. There was a massive mahogany dining table in the center of the room, surrounded by huge chairs uphol- stered in scarlet satin woven with gold thread and tiny rhinestones.

Priscilla Beaulieu Presley entered from a side hall. Her auburn hair was pulled away from her face and hung loose in the back. She wore little makeup and appeared calm. She and Elvis (who were divorced in 1973) had been married for six years. Their nine-year-old daughter, Lisa Marie, had been staying with her father when he died.

"Would you like a Coke or Seven-Up?" Priscilla offered as she walked into the living room, which was paneled in mahogany and decorated with fur-covered African shields and spears.

The former Mrs. Presley seemed to be putting everyone at ease as she moved around the room greeting old friends. She had received the news of her ex-husband's death while lunching with her sister Michele in Los Angeles and had to wait almost five hours before she could contact the crew of Elvis' private four-engine jet, the *Lisa Marie*. She came back to Memphis with her father, a retired Air Force colonel, her mother and her sister. She was the only person in the room dressed in black.

"Would you like to meet Mr. Presley?" asked Priscilla as she led the way to a small bedroom where Vernon Presley, the singer's 61-year-old father, was sitting on a couch with his second wife, Dee. He looked like an older, white-haired version of his son. He introduced Elvis' Uncle Vester, Aunt Delta and Aunt Nash. Minnie Presley, Elvis' 82-year-old grandmother, was resting in a corner chair. They were all staring at a local ten o'clock news show about the day's events and the crowds that had been outside all day long. Nobody spoke.

At the front door, Charlie Hodge, Elvis' rhythm guitarist, was standing near the guest book. He was a small man with dark, styled hair. He was wearing a blue leisure suit with a gold pendant with the initials "TCB" above a lightning bolt. The pendant was a private joke between Elvis and the members of the "Memphis Mafia." It stood for "Taking Care of Business—with a flash."

"It's really hard to believe," he said. "I went to the dentist with him on Monday night around 9:30. We were getting ready for the tour and we talked about the songs we'd use. But we never did rehearse. We just used to make it up right on the stage." His eyes filled with tears and his voice choked. "I haven't really had any sleep. I've been with Elvis all day. Just this afternoon I shaved his sideburns. It was the least I could do."

Outside the front door were hundreds of wreaths; some spelled "Elvis" in flowers, others were shaped like crowns, broken hearts, hound dogs and blue suede shoes.

IT WASN'T ALL JUST GIVING PINK CADILLACS TO HIS FRIENDS

From "On the Road," *Newsweek*, June 25, 2007[*]

By Michael Beschloss

The noted American historian reflects on Graceland.

MEMPHIS, TENNESSEE

THE KING'S CASTLE

I N AUGUST IT WILL BE 30 YEARS SINCE ELVIS PRESLEY SAGGED TO the floor and died alone in the upstairs bathroom of Graceland, the Memphis estate that was his Mount Vernon. This year, Graceland's managers expect the annual candlelight vigil on Aug. 15 to break all records.

Since his death, the aura of the King and the Colonial revival mansion he bought in 1957 has never stopped growing. During an official U.S. visit last summer, the then Japanese Prime Minister

• • •

Junichiro Koizumi insisted on touring Graceland. There, before a chuckling President Bush and Elvis's once wife, Priscilla, and daughter, Lisa Marie, Koizumi mugged like the King and crooned "The Impossible Dream."

Elvis was casual about money, and that is the only reason that the Graceland house—which would be dwarfed by a modern rock star's pool house—is open to visitors. Although Presley transformed America's music, he left an estate so relatively small (reportedly less than $5 million) that Lisa Marie, his principal heir, needed ready cash when he died. Lisa Marie's mother shrewdly hired professional managers, who licensed and merchandised Elvis's image and turned Graceland into a world-renowned tourist attraction. Lisa Marie reportedly takes in a lavish yearly income.

Under the ex-wife's firm instructions, Graceland was remade into a carefully edited public version of the Elvis story. The living room has been stripped of the fiery red furniture and carpets of the 1970s, when the sadly bloated and drug-addicted star lounged with girlfriends like Linda Thompson and Ginger Alden. Instead, it is once again the more sedate white room that Elvis and Priscilla knew in the '60s. The dining room is adorned by their wedding silver and a loving portrait of Priscilla and Lisa Marie.

In the basement, a tuxedoed Elvis mannequin stands next to a black-gowned Priscilla, like a president and First Lady. A Graceland guide says, "Priscilla says she can't remember that Elvis was ever that skinny!"

Displayed in the bedroom of his late mother, Gladys, are the expensive dresses and handbags he bought her—the artifacts of an adoring son. Framed on a downstairs wall are checks he wrote to charities. A guide notes, "It wasn't all just giving pink Cadillacs to his friends!"

Elvis's failed search for spiritual peace is evoked by his "meditation garden," where he was ultimately reburied after an attempted grave robbing, and his favorite, well-thumbed "Cheiro's Book of Numbers," in which he scribbled words like KARATE and ENLIGHTEN.

Visitors cannot go upstairs, where the aging Elvis lay in bed watching TV, sometimes with pistol in hand. Graceland's stewards note that the King did not welcome outsiders to the second floor. No doubt the family prefers to distract visitors from the depressing scene of his demise at 42.

Graceland would be better history if it acknowledged the more tragic lessons of Elvis's short life—the dangers of sudden global adoration and a superstar's increasing isolation. There are few signs of Presley's careerlong manager, Col. Tom Parker, who both nurtured and vandalized him. The management would do some good by warning young visitors against the drug abuse that denied Presley a longer life. The only references to his addictions are unwitting. Among the "friends" listed near the JFK-style eternal flame above Elvis's grave is one of the doctors who scrawled him those many prescriptions. And tucked into the corner of the living room is a green oxygen inhalator. Questioned about this, a guide quickly says, "No, it's not Elvis's! It's there for tourists who might pass out."

As with our presidential libraries, absolute realism is probably too much to expect when strong-willed relatives still hover. So for now, enjoy Elvis's faux-Polynesian Jungle Room, tour his Convair 880 plane, the *Lisa Marie*, and let Graceland send out the happy thoughts that attract foreign leaders and so many other pilgrims every year. Troubled celebrities are a dime a dozen. There was only one King.

When you walk through the house knowing Elvis's actual, more complex history, your heart may ache for what might have been. Look at the stained-glass good-luck peacocks he installed inside his music room in the '70s. "Elvis didn't know," says the guide, "that peacocks only bring you good luck if you leave them outdoors."

SOMEONE TRULY
SINGULAR

From "Elvis's Bad Break,"
National Review, May 22, 2000[*]

By William F. Buckley Jr.

William F. Buckley wonders why we flock to
Graceland.

MEMPHIS, APRIL 18

F YOU THINK *YOU* WERE HURT BY THE MARKET, THINK WHAT happened to Elvis Presley. So you don't care what happened to Elvis Presley? You would care if you stopped by at Graceland, which 700,000 people do every year, one-quarter of them foreign-born. So that's all very interesting, but why the economic blues? Did they cause him to sing a song or whatever about how lonesome he became one day after his market went down?

Even if you care not at all about Elvis Presley, never listened to one of his songs or, if you did, certainly didn't intend to listen to another, he was an important musical figure. But he blanked out in the mid-Seventies from drug bloat, so why can't we get on with somebody else?

• • •

We can and do, but how to account for almost 1 million people going to Graceland every year? And here's something else. He died on August 16, (1977), and a year after that, a few fans began to congregate on the eve of the anniversary of his death, carrying, each one, just one candle. They would walk up and down in front of Graceland. But in 1981 the property was opened to guided tours, so beginning then, the candlelight vigil makes its way in and around the Graceland preserve, passing by the little graveyard where Elvis is buried.

Mr. Jack Soden, who is the chief executive officer of the Graceland operation, tried trimming the crowd down, but after a few years had no alternative than to permit the earliest arrivers to begin their walking vigil at five in the afternoon. By dawn the succeeding day the pathways were drenched from the wax of the memorial candles. Are they older people? After all, Elvis was born in 1935, became famous in 1954—are these old baby boomers who come to Graceland? No. There are still many teenagers who come every day. Graceland doesn't anticipate ending its operation when contemporaries of Elvis die off, which will begin to happen about ten years from now.

But what was his economic crash, that could distract attention from our own free-fall? The man who managed Elvis's affairs was a mysterious, assertive marketer who called himself "Colonel" Parker. He was a libidinous patron of the casinos. The speculation is that when he made the proposal to Elvis in 1975, the Colonel terribly needed some cash. He persuaded (or simply instructed) Elvis to sell to RCA all of his recording royalties as of that moment. The deal was $5 million and the Colonel got his customary 50 percent. Well, those royalties now earn $25 million per year. The bummest deal in musical history.

The same curiosity that brings visitors to Graceland inevitably prompts them to ask to see the second floor, where Elvis lived and died in grisly stupor. The answer is a flat, ingratiating *no*. That is the deal, imposed unsparingly by Lisa Marie, the daughter and heir. Why should anybody want to visit those quarters and ogle at the seven-foot diameter shower in the bathroom and the voluptuous bedroom, an extension of Elvis's resoundingly vulgar tastes?

A silly question: Why do people want to poke into the spot in the warehouse where the killer waited for President Kennedy? Why the allure of the balcony on which Martin Luther King strolled, awaiting the final bullet? Elvis Presley is something of a legend, and it is in very full display at Graceland. There is his pink Cadillac, and his motorcycles, and his big jet airplane and his little jet airplane, and the costumes he wore, which would have dazzled the Pharaohs, and the tractors he bought having zero use for them. But there also, in dazzling numbers, are the gold records he won from the industry, authentic memorabilia of a voice and manner and style that dumbfounded, enthralled, and repelled the largest musical audience ever got together by a single musical artist.

What are they there at Graceland to venerate? An aspect, perhaps, of the spiritual inclination of the American people, who do not require that the memory being venerated should have been a martyr or a prophet. Just someone truly singular and mythogenic, who contributed to his own legend his suicidal ending as a victim of the drugs he inveighed against with the strange, disquieting, appealing innocence that marked his entire life.

SOMETHING
FOR EVERYBODY

From "25 Years Later, Elvis Rolls On,"
New York Times, August 16, 2002[*]

By Jon Pareles

John Pareles, a music critic for the *New York Times* writes about why it's hard for the world to let go of Elvis, even twenty-five years after his death.

IN DEATH AS IN LIFE, ELVIS PRESLEY HAS SOMETHING FOR EVERY-body. Twenty-five years after he died of a drug overdose in his bathroom at Graceland, on Aug. 16, 1977, he is still a charismatic figure, as widely recognized as a president or a Coca-Cola logo. And he is still ripe for admiration and exploitation.

No one wants to let him go. His T.C.B. band from his years in Las Vegas is still performing, with Elvis singing on video; it appears in Memphis tonight. Elvis impersonators work clubs and lounges across America and around the world.

• • •

Elvis remains an archetype as a musician and a celebrity, as an idol of almost religious proportions and a punch line, as a success story and a cautionary tale, as a touchstone for performers and a cash cow for recording companies. RCA, Presley's recording company since the 1950's, and Tomato Records, which acquired some pre-RCA recordings from the "Louisiana Hayride" radio show from 1954 to 1956, both have new Elvis material this year.

Strangely enough, anniversaries of his death are celebrated more fervently than his birthday, Jan. 8, 1935. Maybe it's because they occur more conveniently, during summer vacation and outdoor concert season. Or maybe it's most moving for his public to see Elvis as a sacrificial figure: the guy who came up from nowhere, left American culture all shook up but barely seemed to understand what made him great.

It wasn't only his voice, with its mingled arrogance and flirtation, its doe-eyed gentleness and bluesy sass. It wasn't only his hip-swiveling, lip-curling presence, so potent that when he was once legally coerced into standing still, he had to wiggle only a finger to make the girls scream. It wasn't the bulk of his songs, which throughout his career were largely confined to the offerings of the publishing company, Hill & Range, in which he and his manager were partners. It was his perfect symbolism as the triumphant voice of the unprivileged, a hillbilly cat with his own kind of grace who had outdone countless city slickers and was still, onstage at least, endlessly amused by his fate. Asked in a 1954 radio interview how he came up with his style, Elvis said, "We just stumbled upon it."

He was an inspired misfit. Along with all his natural and cultivated gifts as a performer, he brought a sense of otherness, almost freakishness, to the role of entertainer. He was an oddball from the beginning, wearing flashy zoot suits and eye makeup on country-music stages in the 1950's. And once he was a star, he never became an insider. He stayed in Memphis, not Hollywood, collecting police badges and popping pills. Fans decided to cherish his quirks and excesses, even more so when the tell-alls were published after his death. Graceland, his mansion, is a temple of shag carpeting, platinum albums and broad-beamed automobiles, and among the cherished relics on display is a television set with a bullet hole in it: a souvenir of Elvis the indulged despot, the other side of the king of rock. It only adds to the myth.

Elvis didn't invent rock 'n' roll. That was a collective creation, one he shared with Chuck Berry, Little Richard, Fats Domino, Jerry Lee Lewis and countless rhythm-and-blues singers and honky-tonkers who never escaped the club circuit. But it was Elvis who made the music larger than life. He set off rock 'n' roll's conquest of popular culture, supercharging his synthesis of blues and country, gospel and pop with star presence and a jolt of sexuality. And then, like Prometheus, he paid for the gift he had provided. He submitted to an entertainment business that could imagine nothing better for him than mediocre movies, generic pop songs and a steady job in Las Vegas.

Perhaps he could do too much too well. Decades of louder, faster, more explicit rock have not overpowered the snarling taunts of "That's All Right" or the untold pleasures promised by the sustained "Well . . ." that starts "Good Rockin' Tonight." Both songs were cut in 1954, when Elvis and his band were forging rock 'n' roll from the blues. The growling class warfare of "Hound Dog" and the ardent lust of "One Night" were utterly convincing, but so was the devotion of "Love Me Tender" and the nervous anticipation of "Mystery Train."

While the synthesis that became rock was his most important legacy, Elvis didn't only rock. He took on the Jordanaires vocal group to link him to doo-wop and pop, while "The Million Dollar Quartet" recordings—made in a 1956 Sun Studios jam session with Jerry Lee Lewis, Johnny Cash and Carl Perkins—show how close he was to gospel and country.

When Elvis traded the homegrown music at Sun Records in Memphis for the nationally distributed RCA Records, he may have believed it was time to listen to the professionals who had groomed pop and country stars; rock stars didn't exist at the time. He nurtured his smoothness and control, turning coy in songs like "Teddy Bear" and gigolo-suave in "It's Now or Never." He seemed to think that the wildness and openness of rock 'n' roll were something to grow out of.

Elvis could transcend his surroundings. In the 1960's he cranked out two or three (mostly hokey) movie musicals a year, singing their incidental songs and only occasionally recording on his own terms. For the movies he took on whatever pop idiom his handlers could imagine—Hawaiian ballads, Dixieland, bossa nova—and gamely made the most of it. His voice held its cocky swagger, its warmth and its fun, and every so often he would get some bluesy traction in songs like "Little Sister," "Spinout" or "Like a Baby." But there's only so much anyone, even Elvis, could add to something like "Do the Clam."

He escaped the Hollywood treadmill for the 1968 "Elvis" television special that flexed his rocker's charisma again: wearing black leather, jamming with his old rockabilly combo, teasing the girls as if he had never stopped touring. In 1969 he briefly re-engaged both rock and the era with "Suspicious Minds" and his moment of social consciousness, "In the Ghetto." Then he took on his endless residency in Las Vegas and let himself be swathed in glitter, bombast, self-parody and his own sad girth. He still knew how to work a crowd, and with an offhand phrase or a chuckle he could flash the dangerous charm of his youth. But he was awfully young for nostalgia.

His death in 1977 came at the moment when punk-rock, one of his impudent children, was making itself loudly known. For a while the late Elvis was allegedly turning up at convenience stores in out-of-the-way places. Then he started showing up in bands: Glenn Danzig of the heavy-metal band Danzig, Jon Spencer of the Jon Spencer Blues Explosion and lately Jack White of the White Stripes all recycle Elvis's image and mannerisms.

Pop stars in their 20's still vie for his mantle. Britney Spears put on a white jumpsuit to sing in Las Vegas for HBO (though Elvis didn't have to lip-sync onstage). Eminem, on his current album, compares himself (in "Without Me") to Elvis as a scandalizer and as a white appropriator and profiteer of black music. But Eminem isn't eager to please everyone; Elvis always was. That's what made him the shining counterexample for the next generation of rockers, who well into their 50's and 60's, like the Rolling Stones and Bob Dylan, are determined to stay self-invented.

For the latest anniversary of his death, Elvis is getting a technological resurrection: the first authorized tampering with the original recordings. RCA has already scoured its archives repeatedly, releasing everything from outtakes to stage patter. (If Elvis's death rattle had been recorded, RCA probably would have released it.) This year RCA follows the example of Capitol Records and the Beatles to release "Ones," a collection of 30 remastered No. 1 hits, from "Heartbreak

Hotel" in 1956 to "Way Down," a country hit from 1977. It's a few songs too many, dragged down by 1960's duds like "Wooden Heart." But its collector bait is a new cyber-Elvis single, a remake of "A Little Less Conversation" from the 1968 movie "Live a Little, Love a Little."

"A Little Less Conversation" cleverly revives Elvis at his randiest. As remixed by the Dutch D.J. JXL, it comes across like a Fat Boy Slim single. It lowers Elvis's voice and beefs up the 1968 guitars and horns with a looped funk riff, a cowbell and sirenlike synthesizers, carrying Elvis's urgent come-on into a 21st-century pick-up bar.

"Roots Revolution" (Tomato) applies technology to the other end of Elvis's career: 23 minutes of Elvis performances from "Louisiana Hayride." Since his backup band was barely audible, "Roots Revolution" adds new instrumental tracks, presumably copying the original parts. The reconstituted band sounds aloof from the screams that burst through the microphone in peculiar, digitized surges. But Elvis rides the reaction with growing excitement. He sounds delighted—but not one bit surprised—that he's setting the world afire.

INDEX